Chaos in the Pews
DEVIL'S PLAYGROUND

YOLANDA SOTO

DELAWARE

Book cover design by Adrijus Guscia and Jay Alfred Ferrer
Book interior design by Jodi McPhee
Edited by Sharon Honeycutt

Additional art courtesy pngtree.com

Author's photo by Terrance S. Neal, Sr.
of Bring The Noise Photography
Makeup by Ariel Green

ISBN: 978-0-692-64117-0

Say It Loud Publishing

Printed in the United States of America

Jeanette White, Lanisha Soto, Jessica Soto, Carlita Laws and Sheronda Stevenson, there are no words to express how your unconditional, nonjudgmental compassion, love, and support helped me during the darkest time in my life. I am blessed to have had you in my corner. I love and appreciate you.

Secondly, I'd like to dedicate this book to you, to those of you who have had more failures than successes, who have cried more than laughed, who have been ridiculed instead of supported, and who have lost more than you've gained. You have been chosen by God to go through the refiner's fire. Your pain is the afterbirth of your purpose. Hold on! It will get better. You CAN and WILL make it! I am sending hugs and love to you. God bless.

1 Corinthians 13:4-7
New International Version (NIV)

4 Love is patient, love is kind. It does not envy, it does not boast, it is not proud.

5 It does not dishonor others, it is not self-seeking, it is not easily angered, it keeps no record of wrongs.

6 Love does not delight in evil but rejoices with the truth.

7 It always protects, always trusts, always hopes, always perseveres.

CHAPTER ONE

He, Me, and She

"WERE YOU TRYING TO CAUSE me to wreck when you texted me that seductive picture?" Zion asks.

"No, I felt you needed motivation to get here a little quicker. It's been over six years since I've felt your touch. I want you now! Do I have to get started without you?" Peaches asked.

"I want to watch—definitely not! I'll be there in ten minutes," Zion replies as he throws his cell phone on the passenger seat. He ignores multiple stop signs, accelerates through yellow traffic lights, leaps out of his Tesla, and races to the elevator.

Peaches has been awaiting his arrival in his office at Spencer Investments Firm, the company Zion founded shortly after graduating from college with a master's of science degree in economics and a bachelor's in finance. Zion enters the office, panting and exhausted from running down the long hallway. Peaches watches him as he stands there, six feet three, his dark chocolate, medium muscular frame accentuated by his blue eyes and wavy, tapered fade.

"Are you going to stand there gazing at me all night?" Peaches teases.

"The picturesque view of your caramel body and you wearing those red stilettos I bought you while you lie across my white leather sofa is captivating me. You are so beautiful."

"Mr. Spencer, do you want to make love to me?"

"You know I've never been able to resist you, Peaches."

"Then tell me what I want to hear."

"Yes, I desperately want to make love to you. Come and undress me," Zion demands.

Peaches stands and commands his attention as she motions toward him as a lioness that is conscious she is queen. She strokes her lover's manhood. "Hmmm, I feel someone is ready to come out to play. Let's free the python from its master's cage." Peaches and Zion undo zippers and buttons and toss clothing throughout the room. "I forgot how excited you get when you're with me," Peaches says as she continues to caress Zion's erection.

"I haven't been doing my job if you've forgotten, my love."

"Chocolate daddy, can you help jog my memory?"

The couple stands in the middle of the room, kissing passionately while moving as one toward the sofa. Suddenly, Peaches breaks free from Zion's embrace and pushes him onto the sofa. "What the hell, woman!"

"Shh, this is my jam. Sit back and enjoy the show," Peaches says as she dances to Quincy Jones' "Secret Garden" that's playing on the Bose sound system and filling the silent void in the room. Zion is hypnotized by her sensual movements. The song has played for only a few moments, but it feels like an eternity for Zion.

"Damn it! I can't take any more of this, baby." He stands at full attention with a lovesick look in his eyes. Peaches perceives she has the cure for what ails him and submits to his desires. Throughout the night, their bodies intertwine into positions reminiscent of Cirque du Soleil.

"It's morning, and now it's time for us to say goodbye," Peaches sings along with Shirley Murdock, which is currently playing as a gesture to lighten the heaviness of their parting.

"Don't go—at least not yet. Lay with me," Zion pleads. Peaches nestles her head against his chest. "I've loved you since we were kids. You've always been first in my heart, thoughts, and in my soul. You are my peace in the midst of chaos. It's your smile, your touch, and your love that keeps me sane. Before the money and the accolades, it was you. I love holding you in my arms."

"Zion, please stop. Don't make this harder than it already is. Let's savor our stolen moments. The decisions we've made in our lives can't be undone. There's no going back—only forward."

"I wish I could—"

Peaches places her fingers over Zion's lips. "Wishes are for genies. This is the real world. I could never live with myself if I were the reason you left your children. Our fathers weren't a part of our lives. I wouldn't want that experience for any child. I love you enough to let you go." Peaches sits on the edge of the sofa, grabs her red leather purse, and removes a red wrap dress from it. The dress glides over her five foot nine, full-figured frame as she stands. Zion holds her hand as he walks her to the door.

"I don't want to let you go."

"Zion, we have to let each other go. It's best for everyone." He kisses the tear that's rolling down her cheek.

"She may have my body, but you will always have my heart." The two kiss and embrace as though their bodies need the other to survive. Peaches places her last kiss softly on Zion's lips. She strokes the side of his face, smiles in an attempt to stop the waterfall of tears from falling, and walks out of Zion's life again. He watches as she walks down the corridor until she disappears into the night. Zion then gathers his composure, dresses quickly, and heads home.

⁓

"Honey, is that you?" asks Champagne, Zion's wife. "Yes, I tried not to wake you."

"It's okay. Why don't you come to bed? You've been burning the midnight oil for the past few weeks."

"I will in a few moments. I want to wash away this hard workday," Zion says as he enters their massive master bathroom. He steps into their marble and glass shower, hoping to wash away his thoughts of Peaches. Maybe they'll go down the drain with the water as he bathes himself. "She should have been my wife and the mother of my children. How could I have been such a fool? I'm living another man's life. Her smell, her touch, her kiss, her walk, her laugh, her taste, the way she screams my name when she has an orgasm. God help me! I'm in love with a woman who isn't my wife. Peaches is right. We have to live with our decisions," Zion says to himself as he attempts to exert a minute amount of self-motivation.

He exits the bathroom with a towel wrapped around his waist. Champagne turns over in bed, intending to initiate a conversation with her husband. The intoxicatingly fragrant Polo Black scenting Zion's body momentarily leaves Champagne speechless. She yearns to make love to her husband.

"Damn, he still takes my breath away," she says to herself. "Were you able to resolve the complication at work?"

"Yes, I averted a potential crisis," Zion responds with his back to his wife. The thought of Peaches immediately sends electricity through his body, causing an erection. His towel falls to the floor, leaving Zion's toned assets briefly exposed before he pulls up his Gucci pajamas.

"Sweetheart, it's been a while since we've…"

"I know, Champagne, but I'm exhausted and have to return to the office in less than six hours. I'd like to get some rest."

"I saw your boner and thought…"

"I was cold. That's all. I promise I'll make it up to you, but not tonight. Good night," Zion says as he gets into bed and proceeds to go to sleep.

Champagne tearfully turns her back to him in bed and softly replies, "Okay."

At seven o'clock the next morning, the Spencer household is bustling as the children get prepared for school and Zion readies himself for work. As she does every morning, Champagne has prepared a deliciously hearty breakfast for her family. The children have eaten and their driver whisks them off to private school. Zion walks downstairs as she's tidying the kitchen from the morning's pandemonium. He sits down at the granite breakfast bar where a sterling silver dome cover rests over his plate. Champagne pours him a cup of coffee and adds one sugar cube. Zion removes the lid, revealing eggs Benedict with a velvety hollandaise sauce and mixed fruit on their finest china.

"Honey, I was thinking it'd be great for us to get away this weekend. Just the two of us. My parents would love to spend time with the children. They're getting older now and we need quality time together. What do you think?" Champagne asks.

"I think breakfast was fantastic as usual. I have to check my schedule at work. You know I've taken on new clients. They're demanding and require a lot of my attention. I have responsibilities at work."

"What about your responsibilities to me and this marriage? Do you want to be married, Zion? You're hardly home. The children see you briefly before they leave for school and rarely before bedtime. I feel more like a single parent than a married woman. I need you. We need you. I love you so much, Zion," Champagne implores.

Zion wipes his mouth with the cloth napkin, stands, removes his wallet from his back pocket, and places two thousand dollars on the countertop. "Have a spa day on me. Maybe you can have one of your church friends accompany you. You really need to unwind and take better care of yourself," Zion nonchalantly states.

"Is it her again?"

"Stop allowing your imagination to create ridiculous scenarios. Have fun at the spa and make sure you get a facial. Your senseless stressing is creating wrinkles around your eyes. I'll be home as soon as I can tonight," Zion says before he kisses Champagne on the forehead and leaves for the office.

∽

"Lord, I've been a virtuous wife and I love my husband, but I can't handle any more infidelity. I've done the Christian thing and turned both cheeks. I've forgiven him. He's still so distant. I believe you can work this out in my favor," Champagne prays as she completes her morning chores. She sits on the plush sofa in the family room, pondering whom to call to join her.

Then she stands, walks over to the mirror hanging above the fireplace, and gazes at the wrinkles on her face. The five foot five, biracial beauty with flowing, wavy, auburn hair has packed on the pounds. When she and Zion married, her figure resembled a Coca-Cola bottle weighing one hundred twenty-five pounds. After twenty years and three children, a two-liter complements her physique. Champagne goes through the contacts of her cell phone.

"Hmm, who can I actually tolerate for the day? Let's try you."

"Hello, is First Lady Damita available?"

"Good morning, Minister Spencer. What a pleasant surprise receiving a call from you."

"Good morning to you as well and how are you?"

"I'm blessed and highly favored, especially since I was on your mind this morning." The ladies laugh.

"First Lady, I realize this is last minute, but would you like to accompany me to The Onyx Salon and Day Spa today? It will be my treat."

"Yes, Lord! What time would you like to meet?"

"Is ten-thirty this morning a good time for you?"

"That's perfect."

"I'll text you the address."

"Okay and thank you."

"You're welcome. See you soon." Champagne ends the call and readies herself for her spa day. Her mind flashes back to Zion's infidelities with other women. She can handle that. What's unfathomable is the thought of Zion being with Peaches…a.k.a. Dominique Rothschild, her high school nemesis and Zion's first true love.

Champagne clears her thoughts and prepares to leave so that she'll be back and able to greet the children when they arrive home from school.

The ladies arrive at the spa at the same time. They exit their vehicles and walk toward the door. Once inside, First Lady Damita says, "Minister Spencer, this is truly a blessing. God knows supporting my husband in ministry is a job. I surely need to be pampered today."

"First Lady Damita, we're out of the confines of our perspective ministries and having a girls' day out. Please call me Champagne. I'm blessed by your company. Your 'Women in Ministry' brunch was a smashing success, and I decided I wanted to get to know you."

"Aren't you a sweetheart? All my friends call me Dee. I insist you do likewise."

"Well, Dee, let's get this party started right!" As the ladies snicker, a handsome, deeply tanned man greets them.

"Welcome to The Onyx. Are you ladies ready to experience heaven on earth?" he asks.

"How close can you get us there?" Champagne playfully responds.

The gentleman smiles and his dimples deepen into his cheeks. "Follow me." The attendant guides the ladies through the halls of variating colors of onyx from the walls, to the floor, to the serene waterfalls. He escorts them into a lavish white onyx and mother-of-pearl room filled with white orchids, lilies, tuberose, and dahlia flowers. Floor-to-ceiling silk curtains adorn the windows, and calming stone and mirror water features invoke a peaceful state of mind. The ladies slip out of their clothes and dress in plush white robes hanging on gold hooks that await the ladies' naked bodies.

"Knock, knock...ladies, your experience awaits you." Dee and Champagne hurriedly exit the room wearing only the robes. The attendant summons them from the other side of the changing room. Two manicurist and massage therapists are on standby, anticipating their requests. The attendants assist the ladies onto luxurious massage chairs to begin their treatments.

"Ahh, Champagne, this is heaven. Whenever you need a tag-along, don't hesitate to call me."

"I'll keep that in mind. How did you become a pastor's wife?"

"My husband and I were college sweethearts. We knew in order for our marriage to have a fighting chance we'd need Jesus. Our parents and grandparents committed themselves to Christ prior to their marriages. My parents celebrated their fortieth wedding anniversary a few months ago, and my grandparents have been married for sixty-five years. They encouraged us a great deal but advised it's not always going to be peaches and cream. Tough times came and went, but through Christ their love sustained them."

Champagne asks, "Do you believe they could overcome perpetual infidelity?"

"That's a question I've never thought to ask them. I'm sure if it did happen they'd weigh all their options prior to reacting on their emotions. I can bet my life they'd pray together about it for wisdom. Sometimes we can move too fast, never recognizing God as the author of marriage. He cares about us. When we hurt, He hurts also. I feel indiscretions in a marriage should be kept within those boundaries. Once God has turned that test into a testimony, then it can be shared, especially if you're still together. I'm old-school…no disrespect to you, my dear," Damita responds.

"None taken. I'd like to have a girlfriend-to-girlfriend conversation without it being so deep. I'm a minister of the gospels. I know what the Word says, but can a sister get a hug instead of a sermon?"

"I apologize if that's how I made you feel. It certainly wasn't my intention. Champagne, do you love him? I mean truly love him past his faults?" Damita asks.

"Yes, more than life itself!"

"Have you tried counseling outside the church setting?"

"No. Zion will never agree to a third party being in our business."

"You keep praying as will I. I believe a hot stone massage is calling our names. Shall we?" Damita inquires.

"Yes!" Champagne responds. Hours later, the rejuvenated ladies exit the spa in utter bliss.

"Girlfriend, this has been a fabulous day, all thanks to your generosity. I don't know how I could ever repay you."

"Dee, the pleasure was all mine. I'm pretty sure I can think of something," Champagne laughs. The ministers hug and go their separate ways.

❧

The telephone rings. "Zion Spencer."

"That's a strong name. Are you as strong as you sound?"

"Yes, stronger, deeper, and wider. I miss you, Peaches. Can I see you tonight?"

"No. I'm leaving town tonight. My businesses have me very busy these days. I have investors flying into my corporate office tomorrow afternoon."

"Damn, Peaches, can I at least see you off?"

"No. It's best this way. I'll always have a piece of your heart with me. I love you. Goodbye, Zion."

"Peaches, Peaches, dammit!" Zion's thoughts of Peaches cloud his mind for the remainder of the day. "I'm leaving the office early. Can you cancel and reschedule my appointments?" Zion asks his secretary.

"Yes sir, Mr. Spencer," she responds.

❧

"Daddy!" the children shout as they run to greet their father as he enters the door.

"Hello, my babies. I've missed you. Hello, Champagne."

"Hello, honey. It's good to have you home. I was about to set the table for dinner. Would you like to help me?" Champagne asks Zion.

"No. I better freshen up. I'll return momentarily."

She instructs the children to wash their hands prior to sitting at the table. The tantalizing aromas from the formal dining room entice Zion and bring him downstairs to his family. Herb-crusted prime rib, duchess potatoes, creamed spinach, a salad, and yeast rolls with honey butter adorn the elaborately set table.

The family is seated at the table. "Let's holds hands. Heavenly Father, we thank you for this food and for the hands who prepared this delicious meal. Let us pause before we eat to remember those in need of food, shelter, and love. Bless us all, dear God above. In Jesus' name I pray. Amen. Now let's eat!" Zion says as the children giggle.

"I'm happy you're here with us, Daddy. You're always at work," states his daughter Jazmine.

"Daddy's sorry for being away so much. My business is growing, and I have to be gone more than I'd like to be. Do you know what's best about being your own boss?"

"No."

"You can take a vacation whenever you want, go anyplace you'd like, and take the people you love the most." A big smile spreads across Jazmine's face.

"Zion, you shouldn't excite the children. Your ambitions to be the best canceled the last two family vacations. I'm beginning to think we should plan the next trip without you," Champagne sarcastically states.

"I don't hear you complaining when you're spending the money my ambition has provided for you. Mommy loves spending Daddy's money, doesn't she?" Zion amusingly asks the children.

They respond in unison, "Yes, Daddy."

"Let's finish dinner," Champagne snaps. After dinner the children hurry to their rooms to complete their homework.

Zion is in his home office when Champagne enters, asking, "Why don't you come to bed? I can give you a hot oil back rub."

"No, thanks. I have so much work to do."

"Zion, it's been months since we've made love. I feel like I'm begging my husband to touch me. What's going on with you? Do you still love me? I've been patient. I've been understanding, but I need answers."

"My priority is ensuring the success of my business. I've invested an enormous amount of time and money into my firm. Someone has to support your expensive taste. Don't you enjoy your lifestyle? Your parents thought I'd never be able to provide a decent living for their princess. I've done more than that. Instead of being grateful, you nag, whine, and complain. Is your behavior supposed to turn me on? Hell, no! Borrow some confidence. Stop acting as if you're a weak little girl. If you want to help, get off my case and your ass and get a job to pay for the credit cards you love to max out. Everything isn't about Champagne. I pay the cost to be the boss. Now, if you'll excuse me, I have a job to get back to." Zion stands and shuts the door in Champagne's face.

CHAPTER TWO

Escaping the Past

TWELVE-YEAR-OLD PRECIOUS IS locked in the group home's dingy, damp, and dark basement. A small window allows minimal light to cast shadows within the room. She sits on a cold, lumpy mattress, not understanding what she has done to be placed in this predicament. After all, Deacon Cephas and his wife, the group home managers, have been honored by the mayor for their exemplary work with at-risk youth. Precious fumbles around in the dark. The concrete is cold to her bare feet. The short lace nightgown she was given to wear doesn't keep her warm. She lies on the mattress and rests her head on a single flat pillow. She curls her body into the fitted sheet, trying to warm herself. The door opens at the top of the stairs.

Precious assumes her punishment is over and leaps to feet. She hears voices and says, "Deacon Cephas, I'm sorry for whatever I did. I learned my lesson. Can I go to my room now?"

A man responds as he walks toward her, "You are about to get a lesson." The darkness distorts his face, but Precious recognizes his voice.

"Minister McHenry, what are you doing here?"

He walks up to her and runs his hands through her wavy, long black hair. His hands fondle her forming breasts. "You are so beautiful." Precious' body is gripped by fear. "This is wrong. You shouldn't be here. Please don't touch me."

Minister McHenry pushes Precious onto the mattress, ripping her panties off and throwing them onto the concrete floor. His slimy, thick tongue glides across her neck. He moves his finger in and out of her vagina. Precious begins to cry and scream, "Get off me! Help!"

"Shut up! God is here but He can't save you today," Minister McHenry says as he slaps her.

He adds another finger and begins to caress her clitoris. "Yes, give it to me, baby. You love that, don't you?" Precious doesn't understand what is happening to her body. It feels wrong but it feels good. She cannot control this unstoppable flood of emotions that causes her body to shake and convulse. "Good girl. Now it's my turn." The minister climbs on top of her and forces himself inside her virginal body. "Don't make a sound. You have some good pussy, little girl. Oh yeah. I'll be back for this." Precious cries with every passing stroke of his penis until he removes his penis from her body. "Sit up. You're going to suck me off. I'll teach you. Open your mouth."

"No!" Precious yells. He punches her in the stomach.

She gasps for air as she slumps across the mattress.

"I paid good money for you. My money, my dollar, my rules. Sit up and stick your tongue out. You going to lick me like an ice cream cone and suck me like a popsicle. If you bite me, I will kill you." Not wanting to be beaten, Precious does as he commands her. "Baby girl, you are a natural. Damn, you could give my wife lessons. Faster, faster...play with my balls." Minister McHenry's body shakes and ejaculates into Precious' mouth. Distraught by what has transpired and confused as to what the warm, bitter liquid is in her mouth, Precious spits it out onto the concrete floor. "A lesser man would smack you for not swallowing his seed. I'll give you a pass this time. You did really good, baby girl, for your first time. I'm impressed with you. You've been the best one Deacon has provided us. Same time, same place, next week? Just pencil me." Minister McHenry laughs as he walks up the basement steps and knocks on the door to escape his evil deed.

Precious weeps uncontrollably, realizing this evening of hell will be revisited again. She is startled by the door opening.

"Come upstairs and clean yourself up. You and Mrs. Cephas are going shopping," Deacon Cephas yells down the stairs. Precious hurries up the stairs but Deacon Cephas stops her at the landing. "You better not tell nobody about this. They won't believe you no way. You a bad girl who don't abide by the rules. Nobody cares about you. The Lord sent you here as punishment. This is His will for your life. Get used to it. You understand me, ho?" Precious nods her head yes, fearful of what might occur if she disagrees. "Now go wash your ass."

Precious sits in the bathtub and lets the water from the shower rinse her clean. She has washed her hair numerous times and scrubbed her flesh until it's sore.

The smell, his touch, and the taste of that man have attached to her soul. Precious determines in this moment there is no God, and in order to survive she has to toughen up.

"Precious, be ready in twenty minutes," Mrs. Cephas says from outside the bathroom door. Soon, Precious and Mrs. Cephas leave the devil's playground to go shopping and arrive at the mall. The two have a brief conversation in the parking lot.

"Precious, carry this bag. We're going into my favorite store. I'll pick out suits for church. You'll put them into the bag I gave you. If you're good and don't get caught, I'll allow you to pick something for yourself. Do you understand?" Precious nods her head as she wonders what fresh hell she has entered with these forms of godliness disguised as caretakers. They enter the store and a horn blows loudly.

⌒

"I'm sorry to startle you, darling. Did you have a good nap?" asks Marcus, Precious' husband, as she awakens from her flashback.

"Hell, no," Precious responds.

"I think this move is just what we needed to recommit ourselves to this marriage. There was so much drama in Maryland. Now we're away from our family, friends, bad memories, past mistakes, and by the grace of God, we can become one again," Marcus says as he drives the U-Haul truck across the Delaware line.

"Well, Minister Marcus, you can keep praying, but I'll believe in what I can see. I hope you don't start quoting scriptures. Geez."

"Precious, when you look back over your life, remembering what you have overcome, you should know there is a God. How can we move forward if you don't have faith?"

"Jesus is your thing. Do you. That demonic group home helped me realize there is no God. You want to talk to me about faith? When the deacon was pimping my ass out to local clergy, when I was getting raped weekly on a bloody mattress in the basement, did I have faith? When his Mrs. had me stealing her beautiful church attire, did I have faith? Hell, no! I had me, myself, and I. God was there and did nothing but watch the show. Get the fuck out of here! I had the willingness to survive! You sound like those frauds that raised me. You talk about new beginnings, but it sounds like the same old bullshit to me. The best thing I did for myself was running away at fifteen to get away from them. I wonder if the second-best thing is to run away from you?"

"Precious, I love you. I'm sorry. I wasn't trying to upset you. I don't want to argue. Let me love you and take care of you," Marcus pleads with his wife.

"You're a good man. I probably don't deserve you. I understand the purpose of our move is to escape the shame of my indiscretions.

I'm truly sorry for the pain I've caused you. When we married, you weren't such a Jesus freak. The things you say and do cause me to flashback to the most painful and dark times of my life. I'm aware that isn't your intention, but in the moment I can't cipher my thoughts and emotions. I don't want to talk about the past or God at all. Can we just enjoy the scenery on the way to our new home?" asks Precious.

Marcus contemplates what she said. They have two hours until they reach their destination, so he errs on the side of caution and says, "Okay."

The Farrington's arrive at their new home nestled in Milton, Delaware. "Oh my, Marcus. This home is more beautiful than the pictures online. How did you find it?"

"When I was a little boy, my parents used to come down here during the summer. My mother loved the old-time country feel, and my father loved going to the nearby beaches. Family means a lot to me, so it was a no-brainer to start over here."

"I must admit I'm impressed. I can't wait to see our furniture inside."

"Well, the wait is over. The movers are here," Marcus announces as he points to the truck pulling into their driveway. "You can take it from here. I'm going to the backyard," Marcus tells Precious, who wastes no time directing the movers as to where to place their furnishings.

Marcus walks to the edge of their massive backyard and gets lost in his thoughts. The property line overlooks a pond with ducks swimming about it. "Lord, I love my wife with every fiber of my being.

I'm struggling to forgive her betrayals. It hurts beyond measure. I feel at times like I'm on the verge of losing my mind. Condition me to stand to be the man you've called me to be in this marriage. My spirit is broken and my heart is shattered. Can you put my broken pieces back together again? Father, I'm so tired. You say when I'm weak, I'm strong; but I'm weary. I don't even know what's best for me anymore. Do I stay or walk away? You're an omnipresent God, and I believe you are working this out as I pray. Lord, I thank you in advance for the victory! I give you all the praise, glory, and honor in the name of the Father, the Son, and Holy Spirit. Amen."

CHAPTER THREE

The Power Couple

A NEWS ASSISTANT ASKS, "Fernando, where is Layla?"

"I'm right here. I apologize for my tardiness. My meeting ran over."

"Three minutes to air time. Can someone freshen up Layla's makeup?" the news assistant shouts. Ladies with brushes, gloss, powder, and eyeliner make her camera ready. "Thirty seconds."

Layla joins her husband on set. He has been sitting on the loveseat, awaiting her arrival. "You were cutting it close, my love."

"Yes, but we closed a multimillion-dollar, three-year contract with the state."

"Have I told you how damn sexy you are when you're making us money?" asks Fernando.

"We'll celebrate later," Layla says as she winks at her husband.

"5, 4, 3, 2, 1. Good evening. Thank you for joining us on The Hot Spot. I'm your host, Charlotte Rose. Today's special guests are Fernando and Layla Brown, owners of Quality Trucking, LLC.

Mr. and Mrs. Brown, your company has had an explosive launch. How do you run a successful business and remain happily married?"

"We're locals who grasp what our customers need and want, and we package price our fast, reliable dumping services. No job is too small or too big. Our professionally trained staff is customer-service oriented. We exceed federal and state guidelines for safety and efficiency. We guarantee if you're not happy with our service then the dumps on us.

"My lovely wife and I were college friends. Our friendship blossomed over the years into a beautiful relationship. We welcomed the newest addition to our family roughly six months ago with the birth of our son, Malachi. I'm a very blessed man."

"As entrepreneurs you have commendable attributes. How does your company reach out to those less fortunate?" asks Charlotte.

"Community development and support is a part of our core values. It's our goal to offer a hand up but not a handout. We desire to help those wanting to help themselves but who lack the resources to do so. We partner with local nonprofits across Delmarva who serve the economically disadvantaged members of our communities," Layla responds.

"This concludes our segment of The Hot Spot. If you would like more information about today's guests, visit thehotspot.com. Have a great day, everyone, and stay tuned for your local news."

"Cut!"

"Great job, guys. You both were naturals. It was a pleasure meeting you," Charlotte says.

"The pleasure was ours. Thank you for the opportunity," Layla responds before she and Fernando exit the news station.

"Whoa, you did it, baby!" Fernando says as he pulls Layla to himself and kisses her.

"No. We did it. You can thank the hell out of me once we get home," Layla replies as she and her husband get into their brand-new BMW 750i.

The couple arrives home to find their son asleep and the nanny folding his clothes fresh from the dryer. The scent of Dreft fills the air. They dismiss the nanny early from her duties and stand over Malachi's crib, admiring what their love has created. They watch his chest rise and fall as he sleeps.

"Isn't he the most beautiful thing you've ever seen?" asks Fernando.

"That's my little snickerdoodle," Layla responds.

"Can papi get some of that attention tonight? Quiero violar a cada parte de su cuerpo esta noche," Fernando says as he stands behind Layla so she can feel where he's coming from and begins to place soft kisses on the nape of her neck.

"Mmm, si, papi, steam shower."

The two quickly undress and bolt toward the shower. Their endless moans, groans, and growls of passion are primal. The steam forms small droplets of sweat that cover Fernando's ebony, heavily-built frame. His thick, curly locks of black hair tighten to his scalp. Layla is the love of Fernando's life as he is to her. This voluptuous, pecan-brown beauty savors pleasuring her husband. Their passion for business and life comes full circle as they unite as one.

"I love you, papi," Layla says as her soul mate places a trail of kisses from her neck to her breasts.

"I love you more," Fernando responds as he begins to lick and suck Layla's nipples. Her vaginal muscles begin to pulsate as she gets wet, craving the entrance of her husband. Layla positions Fernando on the teak shower bench. She straddles him, and the rhythm of Layla's hips overtakes him. What feels like hours of lovemaking have only been minutes.

He grabs her hips with his hands hoping to slow her pace, but she's on to his tactic. "I'm about to bust!"

"Not yet, papi." Fernando begins massaging her clitoris with his thumb. She immediately tightens her grasp on his pleasure stick and her pace quickens. She leans back, placing her hands on his knees as an orgasm rushes through her body. Fernando follows, yelling loudly as his body shakes violently. He rests his head on Layla's double-D breasts.

She kisses his forehead. While stroking his back and still straddling him, she asks, "Honey, are you all right?"

"Yeah, sure. Why?" he pants as he responds.

"Well, I wasn't sure if you were having an orgasm or a seizure. I was waiting to see if you needed a paramedic." The couple burst into laughter.

"You are so wrong. Just cold-blooded. Rick James was singing about you!" Fernando playfully taunts. The Browns shower, complete their bedtime rituals, and enter their bedroom to find Malachi has slept through their sexual escapades.

CHAPTER FOUR

Fresh Start

"ARE YOU TAMAR DEPUTY?"

"Yes." The gentleman hands her a large brown envelope and says, "You've been served. Good day, ma'am."

She sits at the kitchen table and empties its contents, but she's distracted by a knock at the door. "I'm coming. Don't take my door off." Tamar opens the door as a white Impala with county tags leaves her driveway. A public auction notice has been taped to her door. She has fifteen days to vacate the premises. Tamar doesn't have the mental strength to remove the official documents from the door, so she redirects her focus to the contents on her table.

Tamar organizes the vanilla-colored papers and reads, "Tamar Deputy, the granddaughter of the late Hattie Mae Pearson, enclosed you will find the deed and keys to your grandmother's colonial estate in Seaford, Delaware, a check for fifty thousand dollars, and the keys to her prized Cadillac. She loved you dearly and wanted our firm to present you with this inheritance. Her only requests were you not sell the property for five years and do not put your husband's name on the deed. Mother Pearson entrusts you to make wise decisions with what she has given you. Good luck. Sincerely, Thomas Hammond, Esq." Tamar weeps as she holds the keys and deed in her hands.

"We can fight this!" Bryan abruptly enters the house, holding the sheriff's notice he ripped off the front door.

"No. God has made provision for us."

"I'm not in the mood for one of your Jesus riddles, scriptures, or whatever. This needs our immediate attention!" declares Bryan.

Tamar conceals the documents, walks into their bedroom, and calmly begins to pack her belongings. Bryan rants and raves throughout the house.

"Woman, do you hear me talking to you? You in here packing as if we're defeated."

"Bryan, the devil is defeated, and I told you God made a way."

Puzzled by his wife's demeanor, Bryan decides to investigate her peaceful mood. "Did you see the notice on the door?" he asks.

"Yes."

"Aren't you worried we're going to be homeless in two weeks?"

"No. I'm not worried or homeless."

Bryan is agitated now more than when he first walked into the house. "Can you tell me what the hell is going on with you?" yells Bryan.

"I'll explain if you don't interrupt me."

"Fine."

"I received a letter today with the deed and keys to mom-mom Hattie's house," responds Tamar.

"Her house down in slower, lower Delaware? You want us to relocate from Maryland to Delaware? Hell to the no!" exclaims Bryan.

"Bryan, I've put up with your lying, cheating, irresponsible, bipolar ways for years. I've been waiting for you to get it together and man up. When is it going to happen? I keep expecting you to give me something that may not be in you to give me. Maybe being a real man isn't in you. She blessed me with this house. You don't have to come with me. I will no longer put my life on hold waiting for you to become the man I wish you could be. Today is a new day. I'm leaving this house and all these horrible memories behind me. Stay or go—it's your choice. But make no mistake…with or without you, I'm leaving Maryland. Now, I have some packing to finish."

Flabbergasted and temporarily left dumbstruck by his unassertive wife's unusually brash statements, Bryan commences to packing after weighing his options.

Tamar begins to sing. "Just another day that the Lord has kept me. He has kept me from all evil and my mind stayed on Him. Mmm, just another day that the Lord has kept me. Thank you, Lord!" She begins to weep as she recounts the times God has been there for her, right on time.

Mother Hattie always felt Tamar needed a change in environment. The front-row seat to the train wreck of a marriage her loving granddaughter had with her philandering husband, Bryan, vexed her spirit. The emotional abuse over the years had taken its toll on Tamar. She lacked motivation and self-confidence. Mother Hattie's dying prayer was that Tamar would get enough strength to leave her deadbeat husband, blossom into the woman she was born to be, and let God send her a suitable mate. This gesture was Mother Hattie's attempt, in death, to help her granddaughter.

Tamar smiles, remembering her final conversations with her grandmother. She is excited to be in a loving, caring, familiar environment. Her hands move quickly as she packs her life's belongings for the big move to Delaware.

Bryan rolls his eyes as he thinks of moving away from his friends, family, and gymnast side chick. A smirk spreads across his face as he realizes this may work to his advantage. He throws his clothes in baskets and trash bags, now motivated by the new opportunities to do what he loves his way.

CHAPTER FIVE

The New Pastor

"THIS IS A BIG LEAP of faith we're taking, but I trust the God in you," says First Lady Patterson.

"I appreciate that. Your apprehension about moving back to Delaware made this a trying decision. I must obey the Lord's call," responds Pastor Demetrius Patterson.

"I would expect nothing else from you. Your desire is to remain in the will of God, and my desire is to make you happy for the rest of our lives. I married a third-generation preacher. You're committed to not only your faith but our family. That's all I've ever wanted in a relationship. Oh my goodness. Look at this picture," says First Lady Patterson.

"We look so much younger," replies her husband.

"Watch it, buddy," First Lady teasingly states.

"The Lord had a plan the day we divinely crossed paths."

"I was a pregnant hot mess trying to work."

"You were the most beautiful woman I had ever seen. I knew in that moment that your face was what I wanted to wake up to every morning."

"We talked for hours as if we'd known each other a lifetime. My pregnancy didn't deter you—it drew you to me. I'm grateful for every day you share with Sahara and me. Demetrius, we're reminiscing... nothing more. Put those sexy hazel eyes to work searching for more boxes," First Lady says as Demetrius beckons her to him.

"We can take a break," he says.

"I have a meeting this afternoon. We can't—"

The Pastor interrupts his wife with a passionate kiss, which leads the love-struck couple to enjoy a mid-morning quickie. Afterwards, they return to packing for their big move to Delaware from Virginia.

"What time is your meeting with the architect and the project manager tomorrow?" asks First Lady Patterson.

"Eleven forty-five. We'll be meeting at the church's building site. Why do you ask?" her husband questions.

"Would you mind if I attended the meeting with you?" she asks.

"I appreciate your willingness to help oversee the plans. However, I conceive the CEO in you would take charge of the project. This is not an organization. This is an organism. The Lord has entrusted me with this vision. I have to ensure it's brought to fruition as He has instructed me," replies Pastor Patterson.

"Okay, but can you make me a promise?" asks First Lady.

"Sure."

"If you feel overwhelmed or the project isn't moving in a direction consistent with your goals, will you then allow me to use my resources to help you?" implores Lady Patterson.

"Yes. You have my word. Can I ask you something?"

"Anything."

"Why were you so reluctant to return to Delaware? I'm sure you have family and childhood friends who would love to reconnect with you. You're a natural at business. Your franchise could experience rapid growth with our close proximity to the metro areas. Is there something you're not telling me? Whatever it is, I'm not going to judge you. I love you with all my heart," Pastor Patterson declares to his wife.

Shaken by her husband's questioning, First Lady quickly composes herself and responds, "Delaware is the small wonder. I felt a big fish in a little pond. I wanted to explore and see what I could accomplish outside the confines of my small-town roots. The things I've been able to do are extraordinary. I've traveled the world, forged relationships with stellar professionals, and have lived my dreams. My businesses have garnered international success. I've been able to do these things because I left my small-town comfort zone. I never saw myself coming back."

"You forgot to mention a few more accomplishments."

First Lady glares at her husband, puzzled by his response. "You're the best bedtime tucker. You give the best hugs and kisses. You're the best wife and mother I've ever known." Demetrius walks toward his wife, who's been placing books from their bookshelves into boxes. He cups her face with both of his hands, gazes into her eyes, and says, "I love you, and nothing will ever change that. I'm dedicated to God, you, and our family. You are etched within my soul. Your spirit is always with me. Do you trust me?"

"Yes, explicitly," Lady Patterson responds.

"Then trust that. We don't know what the future holds, but as long as we have each other, we can get through anything," Demetrius says as he holds his wife in his arms.

First Lady holds her husband tightly, praying the secrets she left in Delaware remain buried in her past.

CHAPTER SIX

History

"H ELLO."

"Champagne, I won't make it home for dinner tonight. It's going to be another late night at the office," Zion states.

"What's going on? Your late nights have turned into early mornings."

"My new client has connections with the federal government that I've been attempting to solidify for years. I'm sorry that I have to work so hard for the house you live in, and for the private school, cars, vacations, and shopping sprees. You love the benefits of being my wife. Deal with the disadvantages."

"Yes, the things are nice, but I love you more, Zion."

"I'm sure you do, Champagne."

"When will we be able to spend some quality time together? I miss you. I realize I've gained some weight. I've hired a personal trainer and a chef to help with healthier meal plans. If that doesn't work, I'll try weight-loss surgery. Tell me what I have to do and I'll do it!"

"I don't have time for this conversation. Pour yourself a glass of wine, take a Xanax, and relax. I'll be home as soon as I'm finished with work. Goodnight."

Champagne's mind is plagued with Zion's past infidelities, so she reaches out to a close friend for support.

"Hello, Minister Champagne. I was thinking about giving you a call."

"Taffi, please call me Champagne. We aren't in church. I need to vent, and I apologize in advance for whatever may come out of my mouth."

"Oh dear. Should I pray now or later?"

"I'll be okay. It's my husband. I think he's having an affair with her again."

"I can't believe he'd turn to Dominique Rothschild again. Furthermore, no one has seen or heard from Peaches in years. What I hear of her is from magazines, the newspaper, or TV. I don't believe Zion would do that. He knows he has a good woman at home. No one else will put up with his crap. You have to pray for him. Put some blessed oil on his clothes, shoes, food, toothbrush, even in his shower gel." The ladies laugh.

"Taffi, you are so crazy. That's why I called you. I knew you'd make me smile. Girl, what else would cause a man in his sexual prime not to touch his wife? He's sleeping with someone. It's not me. I'm not that delusional. My husband is attractive, charming, ambitious, and rich. I'm aware women are throwing ass at him like Frisbees. The question I need the answer to is who is he catching?"

"Champagne, outside looking in, people envy your life. You have everything most women desire to be happy. You live in a mansion, you married the love of your life, you have three beautiful children, and you're able to be a stay-at-home mom. The old folks used to say if you look for trouble you'll find it. Instead, have you ever thought about a legal separation to show Zion you're serious? Women with fewer resources do it every day."

"Taffi, I could never leave Zion. I knew the moment I laid eyes on him I had to have him. He means everything to me. I need him like you need oxygen to breathe. I don't care how many women he sleeps with as long as he comes back home to me. I'm in this for better or for worse. Your worse may be different from mine. Everything I've ever done was for Zion. Our marriage would be perfect if he spent more time with the children and me. There are beautiful, petite, fit women waiting to take my plus-size place. I refuse to give them that opportunity. It will be over my dead body," declares Champagne.

"We've been friends for years, Champagne. We're more like sisters, and I feel your identity is centered around Zion. You should focus your attention on yourself. No one will take care of you like you. If you don't do it, who else will? Those babies need their mama. The calling that God has placed on your life cannot manifest if your mind is consumed with your husband. Talk to him, make a decision about the direction of your life, and let God work it out," pleads Taffi.

"As a single woman, what can you tell me about being married? Do you think I'm going to wash the eighteen years I put into this relationship down the drain of divorce? Hell, no! I'm going to stay and fight for what I've worked hard to get. Dominique and all the rest of those whores can have their flings with him. He parks his car at this house every night. I carry his black card. I'm the woman on his arm at company events and fundraisers. I have his children and his last name. Hell will freeze over before I walk away from this marriage. I, until the day I die, will always be Mrs. Zion Spencer," Champagne announces.

"Well, it's your life. Time is very precious. It's like your virginity. Once it's gone, you can't get it back. My advice and opinion are based on the information you voluntarily shared with me. You complain, yet you stay in this toxic relationship. A man is only going to do what you allow him to do to you. I suggest if you're going to remain married to this man, stop putting your business in the streets. We know he has a problem. After a while, people will start to wonder what's wrong with you for staying with him," Taffi honestly states.

"Go to hell!" Champagne screams as she slams her phone down and ends the call. Champagne's obsessive-compulsive disorder kicks in, and she sprays, wipes, and dusts her home on autopilot. As she reminisces about her and Zion's younger years, her warm thoughts are invaded by a memory of Dominique. "That bitch is always lurking around in our lives. I hate her. I wish she would drop off the face of the earth," Champagne says aloud to herself. She glimpses at the large crystal clock hanging on the wall and wonders what time Zion will arrive home.

෴

Taffi is used to Champagne's outbursts and temper tantrums. Daddy's little princess and heir to Carter Communications has never known the word "no." Frustrated and feeling as if she's missing pivotal information, Taffi contacts Chanel, Champagne's older cousin, who used to be a really close friend until they had a big falling out. If anyone can give Taffi the 411 it will be Chanel.

"Hello."

"Hi, this is Taffi. Is Chanel available?"

"This is she. How are you, girl?"

"I'm fine, but your cousin is another story."

"What's Zion done now?" asks Chanel.

"How did you figure that?"

"Child, please. With Champagne it's always about Zion. She's the poster child for bipolar disorder. So what's up?"

"Chanel, you are the realest, most straight-up person I've ever known and I have a question. I feel as if I'm missing a part of Zion and Champagne's story. When she speaks about their relationship, it sounds like a fairy tale and Dominique is the wicked witch. What am I missing?" asks Taffi.

"I'll give you a history lesson on your girl Champagne. Her parents spared no expense when it came to what Champagne wanted—especially her education. She attended the best private schools in the state. She was ridiculed by her peers for having a black mother and white father. A biracial child back then wasn't as accepted as it is today. She begged her parents to allow her to experience the public school system. They reluctantly agreed.

"Champagne saw Zion and calls it love at first sight. I call it obsession at first sight. Zion and Peaches had been an item since grade school. Their plan was to graduate from college and get married. Everyone knew this—including Champagne. She didn't care. She wanted Zion and considered Dominique an obstacle. Zion initially brushed Champagne off as a harmless crush, but Dominique knew better. Champagne used her family's money, manipulated situations to be alone with Zion, and helped create a breaking point in his relationship with Dominique. He never saw her coming for him.

"A year and a half later, Champagne was pregnant, and pressured by her father, Zion married her. Sometimes you get what you ask for. The foundation of her marriage is deception and manipulation. When you force love, it will never work.

"Zion isn't a bad man. He's just made some bad choices. And now he's stuck in a situation he never planned to be in with a woman who isn't Dominique. She's good people despite what you may have heard about her. A real down-to-earth, kindhearted person. I call her the boardroom hustle. Dominique's intelligent and street-smart. I feel sorry for her. She had her whole life mapped out and in an instant it changed. I believe that's part of her success. Peaches has been trying to fill the void of losing Zion with a ferocious work ethic.

"Champagne is beautiful, pleasant, and very personable, but she's Dr. Jekyll and Mr. Hyde. You're her friend as long as you agree with her. If you decide to voice an honest opinion or try to help her see herself, you become her enemy. She'll scandalize your name, retelling the story and lying by omission, seemingly becoming the victimized party. The portrait she portrays of her life is a beautiful lie.

"Champagne isn't demure, pure, or virtuous. She's a venomous snake ready to strike and spread her poison. I've seen her destroy ministries. Zion is oblivious to the calculating and relentless lengths Champagne has gone through to entrap him. My advice to you is not to get caught in the crossfire.

"I'm sure you feel you can help her. I did, too. But she has to see herself first. That's her biggest mistake. Champagne can point out others' flaws and not acknowledge the errors of her misguided ways. You can't help someone who doesn't believe they have a problem. Remember the long-handled spoon philosophy. It will serve you well when dealing with Champagne. Some folk you have to love from a distance. You take care. I have to go now. See you later."

"Bye," says Taffi.

Taffi is dumbfounded by Chanel's revelations. She begins to think back on all the conversations she has had with Champagne about Zion. "I've been such a fool. What kind of woman is Minister Champagne Carter-Spencer? Lord, I truly need some guidance on this one," Taffi says as she prays before bed.

CHAPTER SEVEN

The Diamond State

"HOME SWEET HOME," TAMAR SAYS as she opens the door to her two-story colonial, which had been renovated prior to Hattie Mae's death. Even though Mother Hattie was not fond of Bryan because he treats Tamar poorly and is unreliable and unstable, not working for months at a time, Tamar loves him and believes he has the potential to be a great man.

"Where do you want these bags?" asks Bryan.

"Set the bags and boxes on the floor in the den. I'll go through them later," replies Tamar.

Bryan walks through the house and says, "It has potential, and beggars can't be choosy. I guess it will do."

"Bryan, I gave you the option to stay in Maryland. I didn't force you to come here with me. This home will do since you were unable to keep a roof over our heads…again."

"Tamar, no matter where we live, I'll always be the man of the house. This is just a pit stop, baby. Don't get it twisted. I'll find us a newer, better place. You'll see."

"Forgive me if I don't hold my breath. You've made so many empty promises. Aren't you tired of lying to me—and yourself? Why are you purposefully trying to spoil this moment? I told you before we left I'm not bringing the same baggage into this house. The dead weight of the past has weighed me down long enough. Do you plan to be a thorn in my flesh?" asks Tamar.

"I don't like your tone or attitude. This house has made you forget your place in this marriage. Let me remind you. You know damn well you can't move to another state without me. You've never done anything by yourself. You can hardly clean the house or wash your puss without complaining about your carpal tunnel or back pain. You're an average female, and no other man would put up with your issues. That dark, quiet space in the back of your mind reminds you how helpless you are without me. You should be proud that a man as fine as myself chooses to be with a woman like you. I've tolerated your behavior due to Mother Hattie's death. But you won't continue to disrespect me in my house. Are we clear? I can't hear you!" Bryan exclaims.

BOOM! BOOM!

"What the Sam hell was that?" asks Bryan.

"I don't know. Why don't you go find out what's happening in your house? I think Mother Hattie isn't happy with how you're speaking to me," taunts Tamar.

"I won't live in a damn haunted house."

"You the man. Go check it out," says Tamar.

Bryan is startled by a sudden knocking at the door. He opens it and says, "Fellas, I wasn't expecting you until later this evening."

"Well, we're here now and ready to hit the beach."

Tamar is too happy about the house to care about Bryan's guests, but she does say, "Fellas, finish unpacking the truck before you leave."

The men hurry to remove every bag, box, and tote from the Jeep Cherokee. Bryan throws the last of the bags on the living-room floor.

"Bye. Don't wait up!" yells Bryan as he closes the front door.

Tamar runs through the house, screaming and laughing. "Thank you, Jesus, for coming to my rescue! You are an on-time God! Mommom Hattie, you were always a step ahead of us all. You got me good this time. 'My opinion matters most,' you told me. The renovation was for me. You sly minx. You kept your illness a secret. It's been months and I still don't know how I'm going to make it without you. I need your wisdom," proclaims Tamar.

Tamar notices the chest she hid the check in and the keys to Mother Hattie's fairly new, midnight-blue Cadillac ATS Coupe. She decides to explore her new neighborhood in her new car. Tamar raises the door to the two-car garage, starts the engine, and cruises down the road. A community bank's flashing sign catches her attention. She pulls into the parking lot, deciding it'd be best to deposit the fifty-thousand-dollar check into a new account. She money is the best money. It's money she doesn't need to tell her husband she has.

⁓

"Hello. Welcome to Community Bank. How can we help you today?" asks a customer service representative.

"I'd like to open a new account," says Tamar.

"Great! Follow me. What type of account were you looking to open today?" asks the service representative.

"My grandmother always told me it's never too early to start saving for retirement. I'd like to put ten thousand in a personal checking account, thirty thousand in a Roth IRA, and ten thousand in a money-market account," Tamar says as she places the endorsed check on the representative's desk with her license and social security card.

"I'm glad to see an assertive woman who knows what she wants. You've made wise decisions. I'll return momentarily with your new account numbers, deposit slips, new customer packet, and forms to sign."

Tamar completes her business at the bank and decides to go shopping. She ventures roughly five miles until she comes across a plaza with boutiques, a spa, and furniture stores, which satisfy her one-stop shopping quest. Tamar purchases ten new outfits and a few pairs of shoes.

Afterwards, she finds that she's exhausted and in desperate need of TLC, although she is enjoying her adventures through the diamond state. When she finds a beautiful building with a modern design and a stone and bamboo water feature as a part of their signage, she turns into the parking lot.

"The Onyx Salon and Day Spa. You're speaking my language. It's time I start taking care of myself," Tamar says aloud to herself as she walks toward the entrance of the building.

"Welcome to The Onyx. How may we help you today?" asks a lovely brunette as she hands Tamar a mimosa.

"This is a great start. I'd like to be pampered with the works!" Tamar excitedly states.

"Ma'am, you've come to the right place. What you want is our indulgence package. A complimentary healthy meal is a part of the indulgence, so you don't end your treatments early to get lunch. Today's meal is grilled salmon with caramelized onions, steamed asparagus, and Caesar salad."

"Sign me up!" says Tamar. She starts with a raw-sugar facial, which is followed by a manicure and pedicure. She falls asleep during her massage. Tamar is awakened for hair and makeup.

As she sits in the stylist's chair, the stylist asks her, "What would you like me to do to your waist-length hair?"

"I'm feeling bold. Chop it! Shoulder length and color me bronze."

"Your wish is my command."

After hair, makeup, and a wardrobe change, Tamar resembles a movie star. The staff is in awe of the drastic change Tamar has undergone in a few hours.

"How do you feel about your new look?"

Tamar attempts to hold back her tears so that she won't muddle her makeup as she reacquaints herself with the new, improved Tamar.

"Who is this person staring back at me?" Tamar says. She is mesmerized by the totality of her transformation.

"The most beautiful you that you've ever seen," the salon manager says as she walks toward Tamar.

"I am beautiful!"

"Yes, you are," the salon staff and patrons agree in unison.

Tamar departs the salon with a new look and attitude, and a newfound love for herself. She's been so caught up in Bryan for the past decade she's neglected herself.

On her way home, she sees a furniture store called The Underground that has one-of-a-kind furniture in an outside display. She decides to browse their selections.

"Good afternoon. My name is Darla. Are you searching for furniture for a particular room?" the saleswoman asks.

"Yes. I'm seeking to purchase a desk for my den and some master bedroom furniture." The saleswoman walks Tamar through the building, which showcases various contemporary and modern furniture. She is introduced to the interior designer, and with her help, Tamar chooses furniture, coordinating paint colors, and accessories. The company guarantees that all the work—including painting—will be completed by this evening.

As Tamar travels home, she prepares herself for Bryan's undermining comments referencing her new appearance. "No matter what he says, I'm beautiful, smart, and more than a conqueror," she says aloud, affirming herself.

She arrives home to find Bryan is still away with his friends. "Good," Tamar says as she walks inside her peaceful residence. A horn blows from the circular driveway. "They're fast," Tamar says as she opens the door for The Underground crew.

She escorts them to the master bedroom, and the delivery men place the furniture, still in the boxes, in the center of the room. Painters drape the boxes with large cloths and begin to tape the room, prepping it for paint. An hour and a half later, the painters have finished, fans are helping accelerate the drying process, and the delivery men have assembled the furniture. Before they leave, Tamar instructs them on the furniture placement within the room. She tips each worker as they exit through the front door.

"I'm finally home," Tamar says as she falls backward onto the king-size bed. She completes the transformation of the master bedroom with new bedding, vases, and wall art. The deep-chocolate tones accented with pale purple and cream complement the richness of the mahogany bedroom set.

Tamar has had a very productive day. She hasn't felt this alive ever, and she basks in her newfound freedom. "The Lord has brought me out and I refuse to go back!" she declares to herself. Tamar then brings her attention to the bags and boxes in the den.

She sorts the items into three categories—trash, keep his, and keep mine—and then places the items to be discarded into the trash bin at the side of the house. She folds and hangs her and Bryan's clothing in the master bedroom closets, placing their lounge wear inside the dresser. Her home is perfect and everything is in its place.

The remodeled kitchen boasts top-of-the-line Wolf stainless-steel appliances and quartz countertops. It's a beautiful room, but standing in it, Tamar's stomach growls, reminding her to make a much-needed trip to the supermarket. Although it's seven o'clock in the evening, Tamar decides there's no time like the present to grocery shop. The neighborhood's beautifully landscaped yards, tennis court, playground, and pond make for a picturesque evening view.

"Thank God. This store is close to my house," she says to herself as she shops.

As Tamar is reviewing the grocery list she entered into her phone, a gentleman walks past her in the aisle saying, "Good evening, beautiful. I've never seen you here before. I'm either dreaming, or you're new to the area. My name is Mitch, and you are?"

"I appreciate the compliment, Mitch. My name is Tamar. I am new to the area. You have a blessed evening. Hopefully, you'll find everything on your list," Tamar says as she points to the crumpled loose-leaf paper in his hands.

"I'm pleasantly surprised by what's not on my list," responds Mitch. Tamar blushes like a cheerleader with a crush on the star quarterback. "I'd like to take you out for dinner, Tamar."

"Mitch, I'm sure you're a great guy, but I regretfully decline your offer. There's too much chaos in my life at this time, and with the move and other issues, I'd feel guilty bringing you into my mess."

"I'm good at cleaning up messes."

Tamar exhales and responds, "My ice cream is melting. I should be heading home. Nice meeting you, Mitch. Maybe I'll see you again."

"I would hope so, beautiful."

Tamar smiles as she exits the aisle. On her way home she is beaming from Mitch's compliment. She pulls into the driveway, removes her bags from the backseat, and is startled by a familiar voice. "Your hands are full. Do you need help with those bags?"

"Mitch, I hope you aren't stalking me."

"I most certainly am not. My house is the fourth home on the next street," he responds through the rolled-down window of his black Porsche Cayenne.

Feeling embarrassed, Tamar says, "I apologize if I insulted you."

"No worries. Welcome, neighbor. I'm pretty sure we'll be seeing each other really soon. Have a good evening."

"Goodnight," responds Tamar.

The attention from Mitch reenergizes her tired body. She stocks the cupboards, fridge, and pantry with food. The house is clean, and the scent from tropical-scented candles fills the air.

Tamar wraps her hair and places a scarf on her head to protect it from the steam of the shower. After showering, she lotions her body and slips into a short-sleeve boxer pajama set with fuzzy slippers.

Tires screeching in the driveway disrupt her tranquility and announce Bryan's return home. He bangs on the front door, shouting, "Let me in, woman!" Tamar hurries downstairs to let him in to avoid alienating her new neighbors. "Damn, it took you long enough to open the door. I need a key."

"Bryan, it's well after midnight. You don't have to be so loud."

"I ain't got time for your mouth. I got to piss."

"You smell like a tavern and cheap cigarettes. You're drunk, aren't you?"

"I'm not drunk. I'm tipsy. I drink because you ask too many damn questions. Go to bed!"

"I will, and you can sleep on the sofa!"

"When the hell did we get a sofa?" Bryan asks before passing out on the hardwood floor in the family room.

Tamar slams the bedroom door. "Lord, I cannot continue to put up with this man's behavior. Something's got to give, and I know what I have to do. Tomorrow's the big day!" Tamar determines in her heart as she goes to sleep.

She awakens bright and early and dresses for a morning workout. Grabbing an energy drink from the fridge, Tamar steps over Bryan who is still passed out on the floor in front of the door and exits, slamming the door behind her. She walks briskly down her driveway toward the community clubhouse, singing along to the music playing through the earbuds attached to her iPod.

A light-brown-skinned, medium-build muscular man with a tapered fade and wearing a pair of black jogging shorts turns and smiles at her as he runs past her.

"Good morning. Are you sure you aren't stalking me?" asks Tamar.

Mitch chuckles as he stops to walk toward her, answering, "Yes. Maybe this is a sign for you to allow me the opportunity to take you to dinner."

"As tempting as your offer sounds, I must decline," replies Tamar.

"How about coffee?" asks Mitch.

"Okay."

The two walk to the community clubhouse. Mitch holds the door open for Tamar, allowing her to walk into the beautiful, whitewashed, brick-and-stucco facility. He escorts her to the second-level cafe and pulls out a wrought-iron chair from the tinted, glass-top table and instructs Tamar to sit down.

"How do you like your coffee?" asks Mitch.

"Three creams and two sugars," replies Tamar. Mitch sets the steaming mug of coffee—prepared to her specifications—onto the table. "Mmm, it smells delicious," says Tamar as she blows on her coffee before sipping it. Mitch stares at her from across the table. "What? You look as though you want to ask me a question."

"I do. Why are you turning me down for dinner? Do you have a man?" asks Mitch.

"It's complicated. I'm working on decluttering my life. The Lord has seen me through some tough times, and I'm learning to make myself a priority."

"So, I may have a chance after your decluttering?"

"Maybe," responds Tamar. "Well, I should be heading home. Thank you for the walk and the coffee," Tamar says as she stands and pushes her chair against the table.

Mitch leaps from his chair, replying, "The pleasure was all mine. Let me at least walk you to your door."

"Okay."

Tamar asks Mitch about his career, and he details his busy schedule as a pharmaceuticals sales executive. He inquires what brought Tamar to Delaware, and they exchange humorous memories of work and family.

Tamar hasn't noticed Bryan glaring at her from the porch. Mitch walks Tamar to the brick walkway of her home, pointing as he says, "I think you have company."

She rolls her eyes, replying, "Unfortunately."

"Where the hell have you been and who is that?" yells Bryan.

"I'm Mitch. Your sister's neighbor."

"My sister…I'm her—"

"Decluttering," Mitch says as he cuts Bryan off. Tamar blushes, smiling so widely her back teeth are visible. "I'll be seeing you around, beautiful," Mitch says, smiling as he looks back at Tamar before jogging off to his residence.

"What the hell was that, Tamar?" probes Bryan as he follows her inside the house.

"A gentleman giving a compliment."

"So you cheating on me?"

Tamar laughs loudly. "You sound a little jealous, boo."

"Woman, I won't stand for you—"

"To what? Quit a good job. Blow money. Stay out all night. You can't say anything to me about what I do! I'm an average chick. Isn't that what you said to me? You coming outside, embarrassing me in front of my new neighbors, stinking like day-old cigarettes and flat beer. This could be the happiest time of our lives, but you find a way to ruin everything. Today is possibly the day I end our marriage. We have an appointment in two hours. I suggest you get yourself cleaned up," Tamar says as she walks upstairs to the master bathroom.

Bryan's delayed reaction could be contributed to his hangover or his utter disbelief at Tamar's candor. Nevertheless, he prepares for the unknown event happening in two hours.

CHAPTER EIGHT

Confessions

"**M**ARCUS, I'VE PACKED YOUR LUNCH. Don't forget it on the counter," Precious says as he hurries toward the door.

"Thanks, honey, and have a great day at work," Marcus says, kissing her cheek as he swipes his lunch box off the counter.

Precious arrives at work to find all the employees outside. "What's going on here?" she says as she pulls into a parking spot. Managing to make her way to the entrance, Precious finds the door locked and the building dark. She stands within the crowd of disgruntled employees.

Lacy, the operations manager and a petite redhead, says loudly, "May I have your attention, please? It is with much regret I must inform you the facility is bankrupt. Therefore, we are letting you all go. Your final paychecks will be mailed within fifteen days to the address we have on file. Further questions can be sent to the email address I've taped to the door. I apologize for the short notice," Lacy concludes as she hurries to her Lexus coupe and speeds away.

Precious begins to laugh as she walks to her vehicle. "If it wasn't for bad luck, I'd have no luck at all," she says to herself as she dials her husband's number.

"Hello."

"Hi, Marcus. You won't believe what happened to me today."

"What's wrong?"

"The company laid off its entire staff. I'm officially unemployed!"

"Don't worry yourself. You're an intelligent woman. The Lord must have a greater opportunity for you," Marcus says, attempting to encourage his wife.

"I told you I lost my job. How the hell did you manage to put your God in that? Damn! Why did I bother to call you?"

"Precious, I love you, but we need professional help in our marriage. There was a flyer left on the windshield of my car. It has the contact information for a new church in Milford called United Church of Pentecost and Deliverance. The pastor is a licensed therapist who specializes in marriage and family counseling. He's offering three free sessions to the first ten families who register online. I believe it would be detrimental to our marriage not to take advantage of this offer. I can't continue to live like this. I always seem to antagonize you. We can discuss it further when I get home from work. Bye." Marcus ends the call, leaving Precious momentarily stunned.

Not willing to submit as the dutiful wife without a fight, Precious determines it feels so good to be so bad. Her thoughts are treading dangerous ground. She closes her eyes, reliving with pleasure the circus sex she had with her lover, a man astutely acquainted with every inch of the female anatomy, a man who is anatomically perfect, standing six feet five with skin reminiscent of the white sands of Hawaii. The shoulder length dreadlocks that adorn his head are complemented by his goatee. He is the kryptonite that can destroy her fragile marriage. With her thoughts in action, she dials his number.

"Hello."

"Hello yourself. Have you missed me?"

"It's my American Express!"

"Yes, it is, and you've been leaving home without me."

"I hate when that happens. What you tryna do, ma?"

"I just got laid off. I need some sexual healing. Can you come lay hands on a sister?"

"Maryland is a hike from this boondock-ass town," states her lover.

"What? You're not in Maryland?" asks Precious.

"No. We moved to Delaware a few weeks ago."

"I guess my luck is changing after all. We also moved to Delaware a few months ago. How the hell did this happen?" asks Precious.

"I'm not sure, but I like it. I'll text you the address to the hotel in Georgetown. Are you down?" asks her lover.

"For whatever, boo."

"I'm going to knock the bottom out of that big ass of yours."

"I look forward to it," responds Precious.

She arrives at the hotel prior to her lover and pays cash for the room. The sexual goodie bag she hides in the trunk of her car conceals an arsenal of pleasurable toys and lotions. She sets the atmosphere for her den of desire: she chooses soft musk incense as a fragrant for the room. Soft vanilla body wash scents her skin. The five-foot six-inch ebony vixen accentuates the richness of her tone by donning a powder blue, mesh halter teddy. Her shoulder-length black hair with red highlights is pulled up into a whimsical bun.

With that all done, Precious sets strawberry warming lotion, a paddle, anal beads, Vaseline, mouthwash, and handcuffs on the nightstand. She then inspects the room, ensuring no detail was overlooked. As she examines herself in the mirror, a knock at the door startles her.

"Who is it?" asks Precious.

"I'm sorry. I must have the wrong room."

Precious swiftly opens the door to find her lover snickering in the doorway. "Don't play with me. Get in here!"

Her lover steps into the room, closing and locking the door behind him. He turns to face Precious, saying, "You're one sexy-ass chocolate sister. Walk for me." She does as he instructs, turning to reveal her curvaceous derriere, which is swallowing her scarcely visible G-string.

"Undress me with your mouth," commands Precious. He obliges and commences to keep his word. They kiss, massage, suck, bite, and punish each other in a gratifying narcissistic sexual competition. Two hours later, exhaustion from multiple orgasms and hunger causes her lover to order them food. The two devour their meal and drinks. They shower, dress, and prepare themselves to face their respective spouses.

～

Feeling guilty over his reaction to Precious' unemployment news, Marcus wants to make it up to her. He attempts to reach her, but his calls go straight to voicemail. Marcus concludes his wife has spent the day seeking new employment. He visits a local florist and purchases two dozen red roses, a large teddy bear, and an encouraging card.

"This should brighten her day," Marcus says as he activates the GPS on her cell phone from his. He is excited to see the smile his surprise brings to her face and imagines variations of her reaction that cause him to laugh aloud.

He arrives at the hotel, assuming his wife has applied for an administrative position, and parks close to the building's entrance.

Marcus stands in front of his car, holding the bouquet of flowers and large stuffed animal, so eager for Precious to see him. Marcus can hardly contain himself.

Precious and her lover make their way to the foyer of the hotel. They embrace, share a passionate kiss, and leave their tryst behind them as they exit the building. Precious stands in disbelief when she notices Marcus standing by his car, holding gifts that are no doubt for her. He charges toward her with fury in his eyes, throwing the thoughtful presents at her.

"I was a sucker to believe you'd ever change. Get your ass home now! I'll deal with you later," Marcus commands Precious. She walks briskly to her car, leaving for home.

"Marcus, man I—"

Marcus punches her lover and knocks him to the ground. "Shut up! My boy! Who told me don't feed into rumors. My best friend who I loved like a brother is still screwing my wife! Bryan, if I catch you near either of us again, I'll bury you!" Marcus says as he kicks Bryan in the stomach.

The front-desk clerk comes outside, screaming, "I'm calling the police if you don't leave right now!" Her statement brings Marcus to himself. He glares at a semi-conscious Bryan lying on the ground.

"Lord, what have I done?" Marcus says aloud as he immediately regrets losing his temper. He is distraught by the day's events as he leaves the hotel premises.

Bryan has a splitting headache. He tries to stand but is very unsteady on his feet, so he rests inside his truck. Bryan contemplates how he will explain his injuries to Tamar.

Precious has been practicing an elaborate, lengthy, dishonest tale. She will cry if all else fails to work.

A tearful, heartbroken Marcus enters their home. He throws his keys on the countertop, turns to face Precious, and asks, "Has our entire marriage been a game for you to play?"

Taken back by the visible pain her actions are causing Marcus, Precious shakes it off and responds, "Marcus, of course not. I'm a damaged soul. They say hurt people hurt people. I need help. I don't want to be this way. I want to love you like a good wife is supposed to love her husband. I agree I need the counseling you suggested earlier. Maybe that pastor can help me understand my self-sabotaging tendencies."

"It sounds good, Precious. It always does, but in the end your true character reveals itself. I can't allow you to continue using your past as the scapegoat for your current habitual infidelity. You either love me or you don't. You either want to be married or not. I'm tired. I'm physically and emotionally drained by you. I thought I could love you beyond the pain of your past. I've been here by your side for years, waiting, hoping, praying for strength and guidance concerning our marriage. I was in this forever. How much am I supposed to endure? How many men do you need to be satisfied because all I've needed was you?" Marcus declares as tears begin to stream from his eyes.

"Marcus, you can't give up on me. I need you! You've been the only constant in my life. I'll do whatever you tell me to do. Those men meant nothing to me. I'm so sorry. Please don't leave me. We can get through this. We always bounce back stronger than before."

"You're always sorry. You say you need me, but you seldom say you love me. If we don't have love and trust, there is no marriage! I need some fresh air." Marcus grabs his keys and walks toward the door.

"Where are you going?" asks Precious.

"Away from you! Move out of our bedroom tonight and into the guest room. We can discuss your living arrangements tomorrow," Marcus says as he slams the door on his way out of the house.

Precious runs to stop him from leaving but is too late. Marcus speeds out of the driveway. Precious is upset, but she has gotten through more difficult situations. She believes Marcus will forgive her. He always does. This time will just require more effort. She grabs her cell phone and dials Bryan's number.

"What?"

"How are you after your confrontation with Marcus?"

"I feel like I've been hit by a train. I don't know how I'm going to explain these cuts and bruises to Tamar."

"Bryan, I'm so sorry."

"Have you seen Marcus since the hotel?"

"Yes, he just left," responds Precious.

"I've known Marcus for over fifteen years and never heard him curse or seen him put his hands on anyone. I really screwed up. He's hurting. He's hurting bad and we did that to him," a sorrowful Bryan admits.

"After the freaky shit we did today, I know damn well you aren't getting a conscience," Precious sarcastically responds.

"Do you have a heart at all? I comprehend I don't mean shit to you and the feeling is fucking mutual. But Marcus is a good dude," states Bryan.

"I threw up in my mouth from my booty call, singing my husband's praises. Where was all this adoration when you were tossing my salad? Negro, please!" responds Precious as she laughs at Bryan.

"You are one sick bitch! I hope he leaves your trifling ass," exclaims Bryan.

"He won't and neither will you! You all come back for more."

"I'm done! My boy deserves so much better than you." Bryan ends the call.

Precious smiles, realizing no man has ever resisted her charms. Marcus is no different. He will succumb to her. He has to because Precious has no one else.

CHAPTER NINE

Motives

CHAMPAGNE IS IN DESPERATE NEED of attention and validation. Since she gets neither from her husband, she turns to the next best thing, her girlfriends. Champagne invites a diverse group of fifteen women, consisting of first ladies, ministers, professionals, business owners, and childhood friends.

"Ladies, thank you for accepting my humble invitation. Evangelist Mason has requested a tour of our home. You're welcome to accompany us," Champagne says as she sashays upstairs. Her guests enter the library. "Zion and I have collected a few priceless books in our travels. An 1884 first edition of *The Adventures of Huckleberry Finn* is a part of our vast collection. The gold leaf, tray ceiling gives this room a regal yet contemporary feel," says Champagne.

She leads her guests to the formal living room where servers holding silver trays of hors d'oeuvres greet them. The party commences as Champagne details the reasoning behind the massive, custom Swarovski crystal chandelier hanging in the room. She goes to great lengths to impress and flaunt her affluent lifestyle in the faces of her mediocre guests.

"Ladies, I'm truly honored to be in the presence of such distinguished women. I am a mere housewife. I love being a mom. But I welcome the break and the adult conversation." The guests chuckle as does Champagne.

"It's commendable in this day and time to stay home with your children. Furthermore, having the resources that allots you the ability to stay home is a blessing in itself. Child care expenses are outrageous," says First Lady Mackenzie.

"Everything is expensive nowadays. That's why the majority of two-parent households work. I'm sure your husband appreciates your dedication to your family," states Evangelist Mason.

"Champagne, are you okay?" asks Kendra.

"Yes. It's nothing worth discussing in this environment. I'm fine."

The women form a semicircle of sisterhood facing Champagne. "It will help to talk about it. I'm sure the attending clergy have held confidential counseling sessions," states First Lady Mackenzie.

They simultaneously agree.

Champagne replies, "I love my husband dearly, but we've had our issues. I'm embarrassed to admit he's been unfaithful in the past, for which I've forgiven him. I realize my appearance has changed and the honeymoon stage is over. Those other women are beautiful, smart, and in shape. Then there's me. What man wants to come home to a blob of fat?" Champagne begins to weep and is engulfed in hugs and affirmations from her guests.

"You can't control another person's actions, especially a man's, but you can control your reaction and what you'll continue to accept from him," says First Lady Mackenzie.

"I wouldn't take it! Life's too short. He either wants you and only you or those hoods in the street. You are a gem, Champagne. You don't have to settle for less. Marriage is a partnership, not a dictatorship.

You have to know your worth. You are valuable. God doesn't want his children abused or mistreated by anyone. I'd take half of everything and start over with a man who loves me. As Christians we accept unfair treatment at times, but being meek and humble doesn't convert to being a doormat. Yes, the Lord says vengeance is mine and He'll repay. But do you want to spend another five years like the last five?" asks a disgusted Evangelist Mason.

"No, but I love him. I could never give up on my family," says Champagne as she walks to the fireplace. For a moment, she holds a sterling silver and rhinestone picture frame that surrounds a portrait of her family, then she walks back toward the attentive women and sits in a plush armless chair. "I want to be in tune with my husband. I no longer want to be clueless concerning matters in my marriage. It's hard for me to trust people because of the trials and tribulations I've endured in my life. No matter how it hurts, I must always be aware of what's going on with my husband. I'm the only Mrs. Zion Spencer, and I will be until the day I die. If I give up, that means the devil wins," declares Champagne.

"Champagne, we love you and will continue to hold you and your family up in prayer," First Lady Mackenzie states with solidarity from the attendees before their attention turns to the new buzz within the community. "Has anyone met the new pastor building the beautiful sanctuary in Milford?" asks First Lady Mackenzie.

"No, but they must have a money tree or substantial sponsorship. The land and structural costs—not to mention relocating to another state—are extremely expensive. We're talking big money," states Minister Collins.

"Well, I heard his wife is an entrepreneur who owns a few businesses. She travels a lot, so I assume she won't be a traditional first lady," states Evangelist Mason.

"I saw the new pastor and his wife standing outside, speaking with a crew of landscapers. I stopped, introduced myself, and welcomed them to the area. They were very personable, attractive, and tall. I'd say they're probably late thirties or early forties." First Lady Thomas has the ladies sitting on the edge of their seats, hanging onto every word she speaks.

"On a scale from one to ten, with ten being extremely handsome, how would you rate the new pastor?" asks Minister Collins.

"I'd give him an eleven," responds First Lady Thomas.

"What color are his eyes?" asks Champagne. Zion's intense blue eyes are what captivated her, but their children, unfortunately, didn't inherit that trait.

"They're a piercing hazel with flecks of green," responds First Lady Thomas.

"Lord, have mercy. I'd have to go to church, come home, and go back to church again to get delivered from my flesh," admits Kendra. The women act as tickled school girls.

"His wife better reduce her trips away from home. A man that fine won't stand a chance against desperate women prowling the pews for a good man. When those sheets are cold and the bed is empty at night, a wife's beauty or intelligence is irrelevant. When that man starts reaching for breasts, hips, and thighs and nothing's there to caress but a pillow…God help her," states Evangelist Mason, and the guests all agree with her.

Champagne's plan has been put into motion. Unbeknownst to them, her guests are working her last nerve. She wants these cackling hens to leave so that she can enjoy the remainder of the afternoon in silence.

"Girlfriends, I hate to interrupt such a fabulous fellowship of strong, lovely women, but all good things must come to an end," Champagne states.

"Champagne, you've been an extraordinarily gracious hostess. We must do this again really soon," states Minister Collins.

"Let me know if you need anything. I'm a phone call away. I love you, my sister in Christ," states Evangelist Mason as she hugs Champagne.

"Stay in touch. I'll be praying for you," states First Lady Mackenzie as she and the remaining ladies say their goodbyes. Champagne thanks each of her guests for attending her modest get-together as they exit.

She closes the door and leans against it.

"Why do you have a smirk on your face? That's the same look you had in your eyes when you were scheming to take Zion from Dominique," asks an inquisitive Kendra.

"Why the hell would you bring her up? You're disrupting my positive energy," responds Champagne.

"Whatever, bitch! I know your ass too well. There was a motive behind this shindig. So spill the beans!" demands Kendra.

"I believe Zion is cheating on me again. These women have walked through my home, seen my family pictures, and made a connection with me through a common denominator."

"Which is what?" asks Kendra.

"The pain of betrayal. Infidelity is a pain a woman never forgets. The remembrance of their pain makes them loyal to me. They are additional sets of eyes and ears unknowingly helping to keeps tabs on Zion. Whomever they confide in will be watchmen as well. Girl power!" Champagne shouts, raising her fist in the air.

"You are crazy in love for real. You keep allowing him to do this to you. If you like it, I love it! I'm honestly tired of hearing about this year after year. Why do you want to know if he's cheating on you? You aren't going to leave him. Let sleeping dogs lie, Champagne. You go looking for a bone, you'll find one," warns Kendra.

"Get out of my house if you can't support me!" screams Champagne.

"You can voice your opinion, but you can't handle your own truth! Zion has been your obsession for years. You've lied and plotted, set so many things in motion that altered the direction of so many lives.

You're married to him and you're still conspiring to keep him. Is it worth having the man's body if his heart belongs to someone else?" asks Kendra.

An enraged Champagne screams, "Get out, get out, get the hell out of my house!"

"I love you, Champagne, but you're a sad woman. I'll leave and await your apology once you've calmed down," says Kendra as she leaves the Spencer's home.

She has never been a fan of Champagne's schemes; however, under no circumstances would she divulge Champagne's secrets. Kendra realizes married couples are two deceitful people. She knows better than to put herself in the middle of this marriage. Champagne has created an impressive public image for herself. To speak against the squeaky-clean reputation Champagne has built for herself is considered social suicide and blasphemy in the eyes of local clergy. What Champagne has done in darkness will surely come to light sooner than later.

CHAPTER TEN

Secrets Revealed

"HELLO. LAYLA BROWN."

"Layla, I've been trying to reach you all morning."

"I apologize, Tiffany. The investors' meeting took longer than I expected. How can I help you?" asks Layla.

"It's imperative that our financials are in order for the upcoming external audit. I've spent the past few weeks preparing for it. Today I discovered a discrepancy that I need you to clarify," states Tiffany.

"Sure. What is it?"

"There's thirty thousand dollars unaccounted for, and I've been unable to track the funds. Have all expenditures been submitted from each department?" asks Tiffany.

"What?! Yes, to my knowledge. I'm on my way. Have you mentioned your findings to anyone else?" inquires Layla.

"No, ma'am," responds Tiffany.

"Good. Keep it that way. I'll research this matter personally," Layla states firmly as she ends her call.

Layla's mind races as she instructs her driver to hurry to the office. She attempts to process the information Tiffany has given her. The past six months have been filled with life-changing events: The family moving into their dream home, their business experiencing record-breaking growth, and welcoming baby Malachi—it all floods her thoughts.

Finally arriving at the office, she leaps from the backseat of the Mercedes-Benz S 600 and walks briskly inside. Tiffany hands her a manila folder detailing her findings in a report. Layla says nothing as she closes the door, confining herself to her corner office.

Immediately she begins to investigate this conundrum. The minutes turn into hours, and the sun begins to set as employees end their workday. Layla tediously reviews the company's financial records, decimal by decimal, line by line, column by column, and page by page. The reports seem to be in order until she notices suspicious expenses for truck repairs.

"Seven months ago..." she says aloud to herself. Layla walks from her desk to Fernando's office, her footsteps echoing throughout the deserted building.

She removes a key from her husband's desk that unlocks a tall, black file cabinet. "It has to be in here," Layla says as she pulls the drawer open with such force that she causes the cabinet to hit the wall. She rummages through the contents of folders until a large brown envelope placed discreetly in the back of the cabinet captures her attention.

Layla rips the envelope open to expose its contents—withdrawal receipts from their business account in varying amounts and totaling the missing thirty thousand dollars. Angry, confused, and utterly shocked, Layla shoves the envelope with the receipts into her briefcase, but she does not afford herself the opportunity to cry.

Driving home, she contemplates, "Is it another woman? Maybe an investment gone wrong? Lord, I have no idea, but you do. Please give me strength to handle the answer," she prays aloud on her way home to confront her husband.

"Hello, Mommy. How was your day?" Fernando asks as he stirs a pan on the stove.

"Interesting."

"You can tell me about it over dinner. My paella will be ready in five minutes."

"Where's the baby?" asks Layla.

"He's napping in the crib. The nanny said he was fussy today. He's teething and had a slight fever. She rubbed his gums with chamomile gel and gave him Tylenol. My poor little guy is a fighter," responds Fernando as Layla takes a seat at the kitchen table.

Her husband begins to fix their plates and drinks and sets them on the table, then he sits at the other end of the table facing Layla. "I'm a bad man! This is banging, baby," Fernando says as he shoves spoonful after spoonful of paella into his mouth. "This is one of your favorite dishes. Why aren't you eating?" asks Fernando.

"I found the receipts in your file cabinet today. It is imperative to our marriage that you be transparent in this moment. I need the unfiltered truth," says Layla as she glares at Fernando.

The delicious morsels in his mouth immediately turn bitter as he hears the cold anger in Layla's tone. It feels as though he is swallowing a mouth full of tacks instead of rice. He realizes he must divulge his darkest secret to the lover of his soul, and he uneasily responds, "Yes."

"What did you do with the money? Are you cheating on me?" asks Layla, interrogating him.

"No. I'm not cheating on you," responds Fernando.

"What the hell did you spend thirty thousand dollars on?"

"I've dreaded this day. I thought I could handle this on my own," he responds.

"Handle what, Fernando? I'm always by your side. There's nothing you'd have to handle without me."

"My addiction," he soberly responds.

"Addiction to what?" asks Layla.

"Cocaine."

Hearing her husband's confession, Layla begins to create a game plan to ensure their business is not adversely affected by this news.

"Do you realize the position you've put our business in—not to mention this is embezzlement. Thank God Tiffany found the discrepancy before the independent audit. We'd both be going to jail. Funds from our personal savings can replace the misappropriated monies," Layla says as she paces the kitchen floor.

Fernando walks toward her and comes to stand facing her, holding her hands as he admits, "I have an addiction to crack cocaine. I need my wife, not my business partner. My wife whom I love with all my heart and soul."

Fernando is aware his wife loves hard and trusts even harder and that his confession could possibly obliterate their relationship. "I'm so sorry, baby. I need you now more than ever. Please don't leave me. This addiction has had me on and off for years. I'll go to counseling, do random drug tests, or whatever you want me to do," a tearful Fernando pleads.

Layla snatches away from his grasp and glares at their wedding portraits that adorn the walls. Suddenly, she rips them from their perfect placement and throws them outside on the ground. "Lies. It's all been lies! My perception of you, this marriage, our business, our family is one big, fat lie! I divulged everything about myself to you. I left nothing unknown to you. This is crazy. You know how I feel about secrets!"

Fernando grabs Layla from behind, embracing her tightly as she mournfully screams, "How could you do this to us? Oh my God, Fernando, this hurts so bad!"

"I know, baby. Forgive me! Forgive me! Please. I can't lose you."

"Get off me! I don't know who the hell I married. You look like my husband. You smell like my husband. You feel like my husband, but I don't know you," Layla says as tears flow from her eyes.

"You know me. I'm the love of your life. The father of your son. The man who pledged to love you for better or for worse. We can get through this," declares Fernando.

"I can't do this right now. Don't think about getting into bed with me tonight," Layla says as she drags her emotionally battered body into her son's bedroom to regain a sense of peace. She kisses his chubby cheeks as she caresses his thick, curly locks.

Layla hopes the tranquility of their master bathroom will help soothe her body. Her muscles and her heart ache for her husband. She can hardly stand in the shower to bathe herself. Layla's body submits to exhaustion as she sits on the pebbled tile shower floor.

The sound of Layla sobbing from the shower pierces Fernando's heart. Everything in him wants to comfort her, but he is consumed with guilt for causing her pain. Instead of going to her, he removes their pictures from the yard and puts the leftover dinner in the fridge. As he finishes tidying up, he notices the silence coming from their master bedroom, and he cautiously opens the door. Layla has fallen asleep surrounded by tissues. Fernando closes the door, careful not to awaken her. He then goes to check on Malachi.

The little guy is awake, playing with his toes. Fernando rubs his tummy and Malachi coos loudly.

"I messed up, son. I broke Mommy's heart and betrayed her trust. She's a tough one. Yes, she is. That's why I chased her. Daddy's got some moves. I'll teach you one day. Yeah, buddy, I wore her down. I knew your mother was special. God made Mommy just for me. Our love created you. I love you both so much. Our family means the world to me. I promise with all my heart that Daddy will fix this. Now, let's fix you a bottle," Fernando says as he picks Malachi up from his crib.

CHAPTER ELEVEN

The Mother-in-Law

MOTHER GAYLE SPENCER HAS BEEN saved, sanctified, Holy Ghost filled, fire baptized, and running for her life for over twenty-five years. And now she is on her way to visit her son, Zion, and her grandchildren. Unfortunately, she also has to tolerate Champagne's undercurrent of disrespect. Unlike Champagne, Zion was not born with a platinum rattle. Her son has come a long way from the modest upbringing she provided as a single parent.

As the gates open to announce her arrival, Mother Spencer prays, "Lord, bridle my tongue and help me to overcome evil with your love. In Jesus' name. Amen." Mother Spencer takes a deep breath as she presses the doorbell with her index finger. The grand chimes radiate throughout the massive home.

Champagne swings the door open and is startled by her surprise guest. "M-Mother Spencer! What a wonderful surprise."

"Now, I'm the one who's surprised."

"Ma'am?"

"Never mind, dear. Are you going to invite me in, or should I return when Zion gets home?"

"Don't be ridiculous and excuse my manners. Come in. Maybe if we had received notice of your arrival, we could have made adequate preparations," states Champagne.

"Child, I'm visiting my son, not the president. I require no special accommodations. Where are my grandchildren?" asks Mother Spencer.

"They're playing in the den," responds Champagne. "Sugars, guess who's here to see you?" Mother Spencer tauntingly asks.

"Mom-mom!" the children scream in unison as they run from the den to greet her.

"I've missed you all so much."

"How much, Mom-mom?" the children ask.

"To the moon and back," responds Mother Spencer. Champagne rolls her eyes from a distance.

"Mother, how long do you plan on being with us?"

"I haven't been here ten minutes and you're ready to get rid of me."

"No, Mother Spencer. Zion generally works late. I never know what time to expect him home. Children, take Mom-mom into the den to play a few games. I'll call Daddy," states Champagne. Mother Spencer smiles at Champagne as she walks hand in hand with her grandchildren. Champagne is ready for her mother-in-law to be out of her hair.

"Hello."

"Hi, babe. I'm calling to let you know your mother is here."

"Wow. What a pleasant surprise. I'll cancel my meeting and be on my way within the hour," states Zion.

"You can cancel a meeting for your mother but not for me?" asks a sarcastic Champagne.

"Yes," responds Zion as he hangs up the phone.

Champagne enters the den, saying, "Children, get cleaned up for dinner. Daddy will be home shortly."

"Champagne, I can help you with dinner. It's been a while since Zion's enjoyed my home cooking," states Mother Spencer.

"I could never ask you to do that. You're a guest in our home," responds Champagne.

"You didn't ask. I offered. It'd be like old times," answers Mother Spencer.

"Mother, you've driven over an hour to be with us. Allow me the opportunity to serve you," responds Champagne.

"Well, if you insist, dear."

"Yes, I do. I'd have it no other way. Children, why don't you show Mother Spencer your redesigned bedrooms."

"Yes! Come with us, Mom-mom." The children cheerfully direct their grandmother upstairs, entertain her with games, and bring her up to speed on the milestones in their young lives.

Champagne happily prepares dinner without assistance from Mother Spencer. She cannot stand Zion's lowly family members and has successfully kept her children from interacting with those people. Even though Mother Spencer is known across the Eastern Shore for two things, her cleanliness and her cooking, Champagne consistently refuses to eat or drink anything offered to her by Zion's family. She stands rather than sits when attending functions on Zion's side of the family, and after an hour or so, she makes an excuse as to why they have to leave. Zion's family isn't blind to Champagne's contempt for them. But for the sake of Zion, they hold their peace.

"I have a special delivery for a Mother Gayle Spencer," yells Zion from downstairs.

"Daddy!" the children shout as they bolt downstairs to greet him. Mother Spencer follows them. They hug their father, placing big kisses on his cheeks.

"Hello, baby. It's been a long time. I've missed you so much."

"I know, Momma. I'm sorry I haven't been able to see you as often as I should. Here...these are for you. The greatest love of my life," says Zion as he hands his mother a beautiful bouquet of two-dozen pink, white, and red roses. "It smells good in here. Have you been in the kitchen, Momma?" asks Zion.

"No. Champagne wouldn't allow it. I'm a guest."

"She's a control freak. Where is the old ball and chain?" asks Zion.

"I believe she's setting the table, son. And I've taught you better than that—mind your manners," scolds Mother Spencer.

"Zion, it's nice that you can make it home for dinner for a change. I'm sure the children won't be able to contain their excitement, being able to break bread with their father. It's been months since we've eaten as a family. Mother Spencer, maybe you should visit more often to help give Zion a reason to leave the office early," Champagne disgustedly states.

"We're in for a treat if the food tastes as good as it smells in here," Mother Spencer says to soften the tension in the room.

"Thank you, Mother Spencer. I hope you're hungry. Dinner's ready," announces Champagne. Everyone takes a seat at the dinner table and begins to spoon food onto their plates.

"Excuse me. We haven't blessed the food yet," says Mother Spencer. The family stops all movement, and they smile at Mother Spencer. "Zion, bless the food, son. I know you remember what I've taught you."

"Yes ma'am," responds Zion. After Zion says grace, the family thoroughly indulge themselves.

"Momma, you look radiant. I feel as if I have to play catch-up since I rarely see you. What has you glowing—besides Jesus?" asks Zion.

"Retirement. It's a blessing to wake up and do whatever I want to do for the day."

"I thought you loved nursing?"

"I do, but health care has changed so much within the last thirty years. There's less 'care' in 'health care' every day. It was time to close that chapter in my life," answers Mother Spencer.

"So what will you do with all your free time, Mother Spencer?" asks Champagne.

"I don't know, dear, and that's the beauty of living one day at a time. I've been doing quite a bit of traveling up and down the East Coast visiting family."

"You've been taking mini adventures from the sound of it. You're comfortable traveling alone as an elderly woman?" asks Champagne.

"Honey, I'm not alone. Jesus is with me wherever I go. You're only as old as you feel. I'm healthy, I have my strength, I'm in my right mind, and as long as the good Lord allows, I'm going to keep on keeping on," responds Mother Spencer.

"Champagne, you set yourself up with that question," taunts Zion.

"Son, the family has been asking about you, Champagne, and the children. Your aunts and I are planning a family reunion. We'd love for you to join us. I understand you're a very busy man, but you have to make time for those who love you. Children, wouldn't you love to see your cousins?" asks Mother Spencer.

"Yes! Daddy, can we go? Please?!" plead the children.

"It will be lots of fun. I can email you the details from my smart-phone," says Mother Spencer.

"Momma, you sending emails?"

"Yes, I am. I have to keep up with technology in order to stay in touch with my grandchildren, nieces, and nephews," responds Mother Spencer.

Champagne knows she cannot allow her children to be exposed to those ghetto hoodlums. Those people are beneath her and her children. "Zion, isn't there an important client who requires your undivided attention? Will they be willing to wait while you go off to play?" asks Champagne.

"A benefit of being your own boss is establishing your availability. If they want what I offer, they'll wait for me. What God has for me, it is for me. Momma's right. I've been working hard for a really long time.

It's been years since I've seen my family. The children are growing every day. They should know where their father comes from," declares Zion.

"I see you've remembered my pearls of wisdom."

"Yes, I have, Momma."

Champagne sends the children upstairs to ready themselves for bed and to complete their homework. Zion and Mother Spencer help Champagne clear the dishes from the dining table, placing them onto the counter in the kitchen.

As they set the last of the dishes down, Zion asks, "Momma, did you happen to bring your red tin filled with homemade cookies?"

They move the dinner conversation to the family room as Mother Spencer says, "I had a hunch you'd ask me that, so I made your favorite, oatmeal raisin, and I made chocolate chip and sugar cookies for the children."

Zion's blue eyes gleam from excitement, reminding Mother Spencer of her son as an adolescent. "Where are they? Can I have one or three?"

"Let's walk to my car to get them," responds Mother Spencer. Zion looks back at Champagne who waves her hand for him to go on. He opens the door for Mother Spencer and bolts toward her vehicle as his wife slams the dishes into the dishwasher, contemplating how to avoid attending Zion's family reunion.

Zion spots the infamous red tin he remembers from his childhood sitting on the front passenger seat. He hurries to open the door, grabs the tin, and removes the lid. The aroma takes him back to summer afternoons, sitting on the porch, drinking lemonade, and eating cookies with his cousins, neighbors, and Peaches. He inhales the first cookie.

"Baby, how are you doing?"

"Fantastic!" Zion responds as he shoves another cookie into his mouth.

"Save some for the children. You know what I mean, boy. I can feel something's going on with you. Don't you dare lie to me. Be honest with me, and more importantly, be honest with yourself," says Mother Spencer.

Zion swallows the last of his cookie, closes the tin, and sets it back on the seat. He begins to walk a little farther down the driveway, and his mother follows him.

"I'm not happy, Momma. I haven't been happy for a really long time. Champagne is a wonderful mother. She takes pride in maintaining our home, and I do care for her." He pauses for a moment and then goes on. "I love her, but I'm not in love with her. I don't think I ever was in love with her. I feel like a trapped rat running on a wheel I can't get off of. What do I do, Momma?" asks Zion.

"Do your feelings have anything to do with Peaches?" Mother Spencer stands face-to-face with her son, looks into his eyes, and asks, "How long have you and Peaches been having an affair?"

"On and off for years. I can't get her out of my system. She gets me on so many levels. There are no words to describe how alive she makes me feel," reveals Zion.

"Forbidden fruit tastes best. I realize your wife doesn't care for me or our family; however, I will not condone you in your wrong. This situation has the potential to blow up in your face. The aftermath affects your children, your wife, and your business. Zion, you can't continue to live your life in this manner. It's selfish. There's too much at stake.

"I saw Peaches a few weeks ago, and there's something you need to know about her. She's married and is genuinely happy. Her husband is an honorable man. I don't believe in my heart she will leave him to be with you. I'm sorry, son. I'm sorry that you're so unhappy with your life, but it's time for you to make a decision about the rest of your life. You have children, so you'll always be a father. I love you dearly, but the grass isn't always greener on the other side. Pray before you make any life-altering decisions," Mother Spencer warns as she walks inside, leaving Zion standing in the middle of the driveway to gather his thoughts.

Zion is in shock, upset, and left speechless by the bombshell his mother has dropped on his heart. Zion determines in his mind to reach Peaches by any means necessary. He cannot fathom a life without her in it.

CHAPTER TWELVE

Couples Therapy

I N AN ATTEMPT TO INTRODUCE himself and his ministry to the community, Pastor Patterson has extended three marriage and/ or family counseling sessions to the first twenty registrants at no cost. The overwhelming outcry from the community causes the church's website to crash within the first twelve hours, but Tamar is able to schedule a session for her and Bryan. She drags her reluctant husband to their first session.

An assistant hands Tamar a clipboard and forms to be completed prior to their session, which she does. The assistant takes the clipboard with the attached forms and says, "Your session will begin momentarily." True to her word, the couple sits in the waiting area for only five minutes or so.

"Mr. and Mrs. Deputy, please come in and be seated. I am Pastor Demetrius Patterson. I see from your forms you've been married for almost ten years. That's quite a milestone. Why have you sought counseling for your marriage?"

"I'm here because this woman wouldn't take no for an answer and so to have peace, I agreed to attend," states Bryan.

"Why do you believe your wife has brought you here?" asks Pastor Patterson.

"For you to tell me I'm the problem in our marriage."

"Are you?" asks Pastor.

"I have regrets. We all do. There's no need to dwell on it. It happened. It's done and it's over. We move on," responds Bryan.

"It may be that easy for you, but have you thought of your wife's healing process? Tamar, I assume your heart is heavy with what you'd like to truly express to your husband," discerns Pastor Patterson.

"Yes, it is," says Tamar.

"Bryan, what was it like growing up in your household?" asks Pastor Patterson.

"My sister and I were raised by our mother. Our father was a chump. He never called or helped us. I've probably seen him five times in my entire life. My mom had two decent boyfriends, but those relationships ended. She almost made it down the aisle once. Baby-momma drama from her soon-to-be husband's ex stopped the wedding. Mom called us the three musketeers," responds Bryan.

"How is your relationship with your mother and sister now?" asks Pastor Patterson.

"Nonexistent. They were killed by a drunk driver my senior year of high school," answers Bryan as he drops his head to his chest.

"I'm very sorry for your loss. I'd like to hear from your wife. Tamar, this is your moment to unleash and speak your truth. Describe what you've endured at the hands of your husband."

"Bryan has partied and gambled away our savings. He doesn't keep a steady job. He's had multiple affairs. The most gut-wrenching betrayal was to discover he was sleeping with my best friend during the time my grandmother was dying. He could have chosen anyone but her. I considered her my sister. She knew my innermost secrets. When

Precious and Marcus lost everything in a house fire, we welcomed them into our home. She sat at my table, ate my food, took showers in my house, and screwed my husband in our bed! There's an anger I never fathomed I could feel. But the soul-numbing pain supersedes every emotion I've experienced. I wondered what I've done in this life to deserve this treatment. Is there anything I could've done to prevent this from happening to me? Does he still love or desire to be with me? It's been me and Jesus through it all. I vehemently prayed, 'Lord, help me keep my mind.' My loving grandmother left me her house. I believe without a shadow of doubt this is my time. I have no desire to move forward with Bryan if there is no change. This is make it or break it time," admits Tamar.

"Explain to your husband what that entails."

"Bryan, when we leave here today, you can put forth an effort to change or pack your bags and get out! I'm not bitter. It's just that I deserve so much better. I refuse to settle one more day," declares Tamar.

Bryan sits speechless, recognizing his wife's ultimatum is serious.

"Bryan, the behaviors that have caused your wife pain seem to be coping mechanisms you use to deter your mind from the root issue."

"What do you mean by my 'behaviors'?" asks Bryan.

"Your unwillingness to straightforwardly deal with problems and your immature and impulsive conduct, for example," answers the pastor. "Plus, you've never had a steady male role model exhibit healthy conflict resolutions, so you create chaos to cope. You can't change the past, but you can learn from it and change future behavior.

"Tamar," Pastor Patterson continues, "I'm a pastor, but I'm a man first. The first time Bryan cheated without receiving any consequences for his actions gave him a free pass to do it again. You have to make him accountable for his actions and whereabouts. You aren't his mother, but you are his life partner. A real man wants a strong, assertive, confident, loving woman. We need that. Take pride in who you are as a person. Don't allow anyone to devalue your worth. How are you both feeling about what I've shared with you?" asks Pastor Patterson.

"I have a lot of thinking to do," says Bryan.

"I have a new outlook on life. I bless God for you, Pastor," responds Tamar.

"I can't do anything without God leading and guiding me. I'm going to give you homework. I've compiled a few Bible verses that I feel will help strengthen your marriage. Before you leave, allow me to pray for you."

"Sure," the couple agrees.

"Heavenly Father, we thank you for these two souls you have joined together. Satan desires to sift them as wheat. You are the potter, and as broken clay, mold them back together again. Touch the Deputys' hearts. Teach them falling in love with you is the best thing they can do for their marriage. You are the ultimate author of love. I touch and agree with them on earth so it will be so in heaven. I thank you for complete healing, love, understanding, compassion, forgiveness, and victory in the name of the Father, Son, and Holy Spirit we believe it is done. Amen. Be blessed in the Lord," concludes Pastor Patterson as he walks the Deputy's out of his office.

They ride home in silence. Once inside the house, Tamar walks into the kitchen to prepare them lunch. Bryan goes upstairs and sits in the recliner in the guest room. The totality of his careless behavior floods Bryan's thoughts and rocks him to his core. Years of bottled-up, raw emotions are released through his tears as his reality check hits him.

"Mom, you would be embarrassed to see the man that I've become, but I promise I'll make you proud of me. God, I'm new to this. I remember my mom telling me to call on you in a time of trouble. I'm in trouble and I really need your help. I've messed up. I don't know how to fix this. Please help direct my actions and words to rebuild my marriage. Thank you, God. Amen."

Bryan ends his prayer and goes downstairs to talk to Tamar. He enters the kitchen as she is dicing chicken for chicken salad.

"Can we save our marriage? Me standing here asking for your forgiveness seems trivial when compared to my indiscretions against you."

"Bryan, I want to save our marriage. Are you willing to put in the work? My concern is you start many things but don't finish anything. This isn't going to be an overnight process," responds Tamar.

"I understand that. I didn't realize what I had until I almost lost you. I'll do whatever it takes to show you I want you and only you," says Bryan.

"I can't blame you for everything. I was so wrapped up in you that I lost who I am myself, but not any longer. I have to start taking an active part in my own happiness. Boundaries will be set, and the consequence for straying outside those boundaries will lead to a divorce."

"I am grateful to God for touching your heart to give me one last chance," states Bryan.

A puzzled Tamar stops cutting the chicken and stares at Bryan. She wonders what game he is playing with her.

"You won't be able to walk back into my life as if nothing has happened. My meekness has been taken as my weakness far too many times. I have to guard my heart. Forgiveness is the easy part. It's trying to forget that's hard," responds his wife.

"Tamar, over the next few months or years, I'll show you how sincere I am. My actions will be the determining factor. I'm so sorry for all the hurt and pain I've caused you. I'm nothing without you and God," declares Bryan.

"I need time—be patient with me. Lunch will be ready shortly," Tamar says as Bryan exits the kitchen.

He is shocked and turned on by his wife's newfound assertiveness. The unconditional love of his wife is all he has ever needed in his life. Extramarital sex as well as sex with his wife is out of the question for now, and restraint is an attribute Bryan has never had to practice until now. But his session with Pastor Patterson brought back fond memories of his mother, and he decides the best approach to honor his mother is to honor his wife. This is a challenge Bryan intends to endure to the end. The stakes are high, and the prize is the heart of his beloved Tamar.

CHAPTER THIRTEEN

Support System

I**T HAS BEEN A FEW** weeks since Fernando's confession, and conversation in the Brown household is nonexistent. Layla feels it is best to say nothing to avoid apologizing for saying the wrong thing. She is sitting on the sofa in the family room when Fernando enters, saying, "Good morning, Layla."

"Morning."

"Has our relationship become this? A few short words?" asks Fernando.

"The fact that we are still under the same roof is because of our son. Be grateful because things can change," snaps Layla.

"I love you. I don't want to lose our family. Will you accompany me to my therapy session today?" asks Fernando.

"I'll check my schedule and think about it," responds Layla as she pretends to be preoccupied with work to avoid continuing a conversation with her husband. A somber Fernando leaves his wife to finish her tasks. Her heart is broken, but the love she feels for him makes it hard to walk away. She realizes any addiction is hard to defeat without the support of the ones who love you. Layla is unsure what the future holds for her marriage, but she decides to support her husband for the sake of their son.

"Text me the appointment time and address to the rehab center. I'll be there," Layla says as she hurries out the door. Fernando attempts to thank her, but she is gone.

Layla arrives at the company as the interim CEO. The employees smile and whisper as she walks through to her office.

"Good morning, boss lady," Tiffany says in her usual chipper voice.

"I don't know how good it is, but morning," responds Layla.

"Every day above ground is a good day, Mrs. Brown."

"Tiffany, I definitely need a lot of your positive energy today. How bad are the rumors floating around the office?"

"Birds chirp. Eagles soar. Don't concern yourself with the opinions of others. It's your signature on our checks. You have to know who you are and stand flat-footed in that truth," states Tiffany.

"I'm concerned our investors will believe the company is unstable with its founding member on medical leave," responds Layla.

"Would you like me to cancel the investors' meeting scheduled for tomorrow?" asks Tiffany.

"I completely forgot about it with everything that's going on in my personal life. No. Don't cancel the meeting. It's essential I exhibit our company's strength in Fernando's absence," states Layla.

"You're an intelligent, hardworking woman. This company has thrived under your leadership as chief financial officer. Your work ethic is unparalleled to anyone else I've met—male or female. As CEO, you'll exceed the investors' and your own expectations. Have more faith in your abilities to lead us," declares Tiffany.

"I wish I could bottle your positivity. I truly appreciate your encouraging words. I'll be leaving early today. Please reschedule my afternoon appointments," says Layla.

"Your afternoons have been cleared for the next two weeks. I determined you'd need more time to get settled into your new position. I hope you don't mind," states Tiffany.

"No. I appreciate you taking the initiative to plan ahead for me," responds Layla. The two review the company's financials for the upcoming investors' meeting. The reports are flawless now. "Tiffany, prepare the documents for the presentation and include an agenda. A thirty-five percent increase in profit margins within the last year should satisfy our investors," says Layla.

"Yes ma'am. Is there anything else I can do for you?" asks Tiffany.

"No. I'll be leaving shortly to meet Fernando. Thank you for your dedication and stepping up during our time of transition," replies Layla.

"Any time," Tiffany responds as she leaves Layla's office. Layla finishes up a few loose ends as she prepares herself for the counseling session with her husband.

Fernando paces in the waiting room as he awaits Layla's arrival. "Lord, please help me to help myself and my wife," he says aloud to himself. A smile spreads across Fernando's face as his beautiful wife enters the building. "You made it."

"Yes, I said I'd be here. What's next?" asks Layla.

"I've already signed us in. They should be calling us shortly. Thank you, Layla."

She doesn't respond and instead turns her back toward him to gaze out of the massive, slightly tinted window. The multistory, brick facility is beautifully landscaped with lush greenery. The warm breeze fills the air with the soothing fragrance of lavender, which is planted around the building. The unique rock-and-water feature invokes a peaceful calm. Layla zones out into her thoughts and doesn't hear her name being called by the medical assistant.

"Mrs. Brown," repeats the young woman.

"Honey." Fernando's voice snaps her back to the reality of where she is in this moment.

"I'm sorry," states Layla.

"It's okay. Follow me, Mr. and Mrs. Brown," says the assistant, who then escorts them to a modern, custom-designed room.

A tall, thin, light-skinned black man wearing a form-fitting suit with thick, round glasses greets them as they enter. "Good to see you, Fernando. This must be your beautiful wife, Layla. I've heard amazing things about you. My name is Baron Monroe."

"Good afternoon, Mr. Monroe," Layla says as she shakes his hand.

"Please, have a seat and let's begin. Fernando, I'd like to congratulate you for passing your last two random drug tests. Keep up the good work. Continue to take it one day at a time. How is your outlook regarding your life?" asks Baron.

"I believe anything is possible with God and the love of a good woman by my side. I pray our love can get us through this," answers Fernando.

"Layla, it's imperative that you understand you can make or break Fernando's recovery. How big or small of a role you play in helping him overcome his addiction is important. This can be an immense undertaking, supporting a recovering addict," states Baron.

"You will not make this about me. I'm the drug free one—remember? I refuse to accept my actions as a trigger for my husband to embezzle money from our business so that he can buy drugs!

I get angry and upset. Terrible things can happen in life. Where is his accountability for his own actions? If this is the psychobabble bullshit you're feeding him, I understand why his expectations are high. I'm coping and dealing with the aftermath of his betrayal without being under the influence of anything besides prayer. You have to come better than this when talking to me. You prove common sense doesn't come in a book. Where is Ashton because I know I'm being punked right now," a disgusted Layla firmly states.

"Honey, please," pleads Fernando. "You now see what I'm dealing with, Baron. I love you more than any woman I've ever known, Layla. This is only a test. We can pass it together," Fernando says as he begins to weep. Layla's heart aches to comfort him, but she cannot submit to her emotions.

"Layla, this is not psychobabble bullshit. Your husband's life is at stake. Whether you remain married or not, he has to stay clean. You may not want to admit it, but you're a trigger for him. He's so caught up in pleasing you and making you happy he neglects himself. Fernando has to come first in order to survive," stresses Baron.

"I will do whatever I can to help him, but he has to help himself. I will not be the scapegoat for him wanting to use drugs. Stressful situations will arise. He has to be able to adapt or withdraw himself. It's my understanding that the purpose of him seeing you is to equip him with the tools, strategies, and life skills he needs to overcome his addiction. All I've heard are excuses and a lot of breastfeeding for his self-destructive behavior. We have a business and a family. Life will continue to bring challenges. There's never an excuse big enough to warrant drug abuse. My childhood wasn't the best. Education was my drug of choice. I aspired to be more and didn't allow my environment to dictate my outcome," responds Layla.

"Everyone isn't as strong-willed as you. There are people who need a little more help and attention. Some people can press through adversity and others struggle. Our differences, strengths, and weaknesses make us all unique. Fernando needs a solid support system. Your opinion trumps what anyone else thinks or says about him. That's a lot of power to have over an individual," states Baron.

"I haven't sprinkled fairy dust over his head. He wouldn't be fighting this addiction if I had that much power, and I sure as hell wouldn't be here talking to you. I'm done with this cotton-candy therapy session! Fernando, I'm going back to work," Layla announces as she grabs her purse, slamming the door as she leaves Baron's office.

Fernando remains seated on the stiff, brown leather sofa. "It's obvious your wife loves you deeply. This is a lot harder for her to digest than she'll admit to you. Do you honestly feel your wife can forgive you moving forward in your marriage?" asks Baron.

"I want to believe she can, but she's so angry."

"Your actions have to be in-line with what comes out of your mouth. You have a good woman, Fernando. Be patient with her. If you want to keep your family, keep your word to her."

"Baron, I plan on doing just that."

CHAPTER FOURTEEN

Peaches Is M. J. A.

MOTHER SPENCER'S BOMBSHELL VISIT HAS left Zion distraught and anxious to speak with Peaches. The thought of another man capturing the heart of his lifelong love is nauseating. Zion sits in his office, unable to concentrate on work. Memories flood his thoughts. His recollection of the lovemaking session they had in his office is too much to handle.

He calls his assistant. "Carly, clear my schedule and contact my pilot. Tell him to be ready within the hour. I'll provide instructions on my way to the airstrip."

"Yes sir, Mr. Spencer."

He decides to call Champagne to avoid receiving a call from her later.

"Hello."

"Hi, Champagne. I have bad news. I have an unexpected business trip. One of my principal investors is threatening to take his business to a rival firm. I'm flying to his corporate office to persuade him to remain a valuable client."

"I'm not surprised, Zion. All you do is work, work, and more work. Maybe one day you'll have time for your children," snaps Champagne.

"I didn't call to argue. See you soon and kiss the children good-night for me."

"Whatever. We'll be fine. Go take care of your business," Champagne says as she abruptly hangs up the phone.

This is a tiresome game Zion no longer wishes to play, but for the sake of the children, he has stayed with Champagne. His pulse is racing and his heart feels as though it will jump out of his chest. He seems to leap onto the private jet.

"Where are we headed, sir?" asks the pilot.

"Virginia. We're headed to Virginia as fast as we can get there."

"Yes sir, Mr. Spencer. I'll notify dispatch of our flight plan," responds the pilot.

Zion's body goes limp as he sits on a leather massage seat. While awaiting takeoff, Zion sends Peaches numerous emails.

The pilot returns from the cockpit, saying, "We'll depart within thirty minutes."

"Great!" Zion responds as he makes calls to her offices across the tristate area. Peaches can be anywhere at any moment. That is the beauty of their relationship, the excitement and spontaneity of their torrid romance.

"Dammit, Peaches, respond! Where are you? I need you," Zion says aloud to himself. From his wallet, he removes a picture of Peaches he's hidden behind his license. "Who is the man that caused such a force of nature to commit herself to him?" Zion contemplates that this man is exceptionally special. He wonders what Mother Spencer knows about her husband that she didn't reveal to him.

❧

"We'll be landing in ten minutes," the pilot announces over the intercom. Those few hours in flight seemed as minutes.

Zion deplanes and hurries inside the awaiting car. "Rothschild Enterprises and please…hurry!" demands Zion as he hands the driver two hundred-dollar bills.

"Yes sir, Mr. Spencer." The driver speeds off to his assigned destination as Zion plays various scenarios in his mind.

"What if her husband is there? What if she doesn't want to see me? I have to risk it all to be in her presence one more time. I want you and only you for the rest of my life. I have to make her understand. Momma has to be wrong!" Zion says to himself as he prepares for this unpredictable encounter with Peaches.

"We're here, sir," says the driver.

"Thank you," Zion says as he sprints toward the fifteen-story, glass-and-steel office building.

He bursts into the office building and startles the receptionist. Her disturbed facial expression prompts the security guard to come to her aid.

The guard stands next to the receptionist's desk and asks, "Who are you here to see?"

Gasping for his next breath, Zion responds, "Dominique Rothschild."

"Do you have an appointment to see Ms. Rothschild?" asks the guard.

Zion regains his composure, feeling full of himself, and replies, "I am Zion Spencer, president of Spencer Investments Firm. I don't need an appointment. We've been business colleagues for over ten years and friends for twenty-five. I suggest you send me to the tenth floor to her assistant, Valerie, if you want to keep your job."

"I apologize, Mr. Spencer. I didn't realize…"

"Well, you know now, Randy. I'm going to Ms. Rothschild's office. I'll give you the privilege of escorting me. This indiscretion can remain between us. What do you say?" Zion states smugly as he walks past the guard after reading his name badge.

"Follow me, sir." Randy leads the way to Peaches' office.

"Valerie, Mr. Spencer is here to see Ms. Rothschild. Have a great day, sir," says the guard as he walks back toward the elevator.

"Mr. Spencer, it's good to see you. How have you been?" asks Valerie.

"Fine. Valerie, I really need to speak with Dominique. Is she in her office?" Zion asks frantically.

"No. She's out of the office working on a new project with her husband. She's left a report for you to review. She'll be on hiatus for the next four weeks. Her VP is available for additional information," Valerie responds as she hands Zion a sealed, legal-size envelope.

"Thank you," he replies as he accepts the envelope. Zion leaves the building, walks to a nearby park, and empties the contents of the envelope on the bench. The scent of Peaches' perfume escapes the envelope. It is a letter.

Dear Zion,

I'm sure by now you've learned I'm a married woman. I have been for some time now. He's a good man. I don't deserve him. I was married the last time we made love. The crushing guilt I feel convicts me. I can no longer be the one you turn to. I can no longer betray my husband's trust.

From the time I was a little girl, I believed I would be the one people referred to as Mrs. Zion Spencer, but Champagne came in like a whirlwind. You got caught up and I got left on the sideline. When she no longer captivated your attention,

I was there for you. I didn't realize how much I was settling until my husband came into my life.

He gave me new dreams and a new last name. This may be hard for you to accept, but I have to make you understand. He makes me feel like his queen. He adores me, and in a room full of beautiful women, he sees only me. I'm the center of his world. He rescued me from an existence of just enough and has given me an abundance of living my life. I've met his family, friends, and colleagues. I'm not whisked away to be hidden as a secret. He proudly parades me on his arm.

I don't blame you. I was a willing participant. Now, though, what's best for me is to not be with you. We share many beautiful memories, and I'll always have a part of you with me. If you aren't happy in your marriage, end it or fix it. You chose a life without me. It's my choice to finally let you go.

Goodbye, Zion

Random emotions flood Zion's mind, body, and soul. He runs to a vacant area of the park, falls to his knees, and releases bloodcurdling bellows. "I'm too late! I've lost her! Oh God, what have I done?" he screams as tears flow heavily down his face. He lays heartbroken in the grass. The setting sun confirms the realization of a tomorrow without Peaches. Zion compels himself to contact his driver who takes him back to the jet to go home.

❧

Champagne has put the children to bed. The fragrant, baked-apple candles welcome him home. He walks to the bar, snatches a stemless brandy glass, and fills it with cognac. He gulps down the eighty-proof spirit, refills the glass, drinks all the contents, and slams the empty glass on the bar top. Frustrated by the day's events, Zion flings the bedroom door open.

"What the…? Zion, I wasn't expecting you. How was your trip?" asks Champagne.

"My procrastination led to the loss of an irreplaceable client to a competitor."

"I'm sorry to hear that. I know you've been working overtime to be the best."

"Do you remember when I said I'd make it up to you? Well, tonight's the night!" Zion says, and without warning, he removes the blankets that were covering Champagne's body. He leaves his clothes in a pile on the floor then climbs on top of his wife, spreading her legs apart, and forces himself inside her. She screams from the pain and pleasure as he pounds into her. This isn't the normal manner in which they are intimate. Champagne savors every thrust, stroke, and touch from her husband. She has a body-shaking orgasm, and Zion follows shortly after her. Champagne attempts to kiss him, but he turns his face away from her.

"I'm taking a shower," Zion says as he gets out of bed.

"Okay." The smell of Zion on her skin and in her is intoxicating. She will shower in the morning.

Zion wants to abide by Peaches' wishes, but the love he feels for her won't allow him to. "I know you say it's over, but I won't stop searching until I find you," declares Zion in his heart as he washes the scent of Champagne from his body.

CHAPTER FIFTEEN

Church Celebration

Today is the day Pastor Demetrius Patterson's vision lead by God has come to fruition. First Lady is delegating staff to help ease her husband's nerves. Unfortunately, she will not be able to attend the entire ceremony due to a business-related emergency.

"Sweetheart," says First Lady as she enters her husband's study, "I feel terrible about leaving you today of all days."

"When I married you, I knew you were a beautiful, driven, smart entrepreneur. This is about God, not me. I'm just a willing vessel He chose to use. We will have plenty of opportunities to celebrate," states Pastor Patterson.

"Have I told you today how much I love you?" asks Lady Patterson.

"Yes, but I never tire of hearing it," responds her husband. First Lady softly kisses Pastor Patterson on the lips. "Have mercy, Jesus! Babe, you're waking up my flesh. I need to be in the spirit to hear from the Lord," states Pastor Patterson.

"Well, I'm off to attend to my business. We can pick up where we left off when I return home."

"Definitely!" responds Pastor Patterson.

"Sahara is sitting on the front row with the nanny. I'll stay for the beginning of the ceremony. I should be home by midnight. If anything changes, I'll call you. I'm so proud of you," First Lady says as she hugs her husband before leaving the study.

⟨⟩

Pastor Patterson prays and meditates in preparation for his first sermon as the overseer of the United Church of Pentecost and Deliverance Ministries. First Lady has outdone herself marketing the grand church unveiling to the community. The mayor, city council members, and clergy from across the mid-Atlantic and Eastern Shore have all come to support the great work Pastor Patterson's reputation precedes.

Bryan and Tamar arrive, take their seats, and await the start of the program. "I know Pastor is going to deliver a powerful word!" says Tamar.

"I'm going to hold onto my seat!" responds Bryan as they both chuckle.

Champagne unenthusiastically accepted First Lady Mackenzie's invitation to the church celebration. The fact that she has to endure the sound of Mother Gayle Spencer presiding over the service is daunting. In an effort to appease his mother, Zion agrees to support her. Minister Champagne Spencer is dressed to impress. Her elegant, two-piece, knee-length peach suit is accented with a diamond belt. Her coordinating hat is adorned with a broach similar to her belt. The children are dressed in complementary shades of peach. Zion's cream suit is enhanced by a peach tie and handkerchief. Public image is everything to Champagne.

"What time is this service going to end?" asks Champagne.

"I have no idea. I'd think you'd want me in church as much as possible. It's been a while since I've been in the house of the Lord, Minister," sarcastically states Zion.

"I only ask because the children generally get restless after two hours."

"If you or the children get restless, take the car. I'll call my driver. I'm not leaving early. I'll support my mother tonight," responds Zion.

Fernando and Layla arrive in desperate need of a spiritual breakthrough and deliverance. The postcard announcement they received in the mail could not have arrived at a better time. The Browns sit on an end row toward the back left of the sanctuary.

"Layla, I want to thank you for agreeing to attend this service with me."

"I'm sure the Lord realizes we need Him with everything that has transpired within the past few months."

"I've heard a lot of great things about this pastor," says Fernando.

"This program is going to be amazing! They have some of the best gospel talent in Delmarva performing today. Oh my goodness, Mother Spencer is the Mistress of Ceremonies. I haven't seen her in years," states an excited Layla.

"Isn't that the lady who makes those delicious yeast rolls and rice pudding?"

"Yes. She's the church mother of Breaking Chains Outreach Ministries," responds Layla.

"Do you think they'll be serving after the service? I can taste one of her rolls now. My mouth is watering thinking about them. I wonder if she brought a few rolls with her. I need them in my life," Fernando says with a big smile. He and Layla share a laugh.

"You're always ready to bite something," jokingly states Layla.

"It does my heart good to hear you laugh and to see you smile," admits Fernando. The Browns attentively observe local celebrities and politicians make their entrance into the beautiful edifice.

Precious is working every angle to convince Marcus she is a changed woman. A flyer she received at the local nail shop announcing the church's celebration prompted Precious to ask Marcus to attend with her. He is not buying her act but realizes a real Holy Ghost encounter can purge Precious of her dreadful conduct. He agreed to her request. When they arrive, Marcus greets fellow clergymen who whisper and point at Precious as they take their seats in the balcony.

Ushers escort clergy and their spouses to the front left of the church to be seated. Apostles, bishops, and pastors are ushered to the pulpit to be seated. Demetrius' father, Bishop Clarence Patterson, has always been supportive of his son's endeavors. A voice resonates throughout the sanctuary.

"Praise the Lord, everybody. Praise the Lord. How many know ain't no party like a Holy Ghost party because a Holy Ghost party can't stop, won't stop. Amen!" Mother Spencer says as the audience cheers and laugh. "That was a shout-out to the young people. Precious hearts, I stand before you, giving honor to God who is the head of my life. My pastor, in his absence, the clergy in their respective places, and of course this wonderful man of God we are here to celebrate, Pastor Demetrius Patterson and his wife in her absence. Let's stand and give honor to whom it is due. This man has a heart for people, and we bless God for him today." The applause from the packed-to-capacity edifice sounds as thunder. The attendees take their seats. "We will open the service with 'This Is the Day,' a good old congregational song. Following that, we'll have opening prayer by Minister Collins," says Mother Spencer as she leads the parishioners in singing a few choruses before handing the microphone to Minister Collins.

"Father, we thank you that you have been with us all last week and that your presence is with us now. We gladly surrender to you in worship and in praise. For those who are sick, we ask for healing. For those on their way, we ask for traveling mercy.

"We invite your Holy Spirit to move freely amongst us. Equip us, challenge us, comfort us, teach us, inspire us, and open our ears so we may hear your voice. Open our minds so we may receive your eternal wisdom. Open our spirits so we may know your leading and guidance. Open our hearts so we may receive your love. Lord, we thank you for Pastor Patterson. We pray that you give him great inspiration as he shares what you have placed in his heart. We ask all this in the glorious name of Jesus. Amen." Minister Collins concludes the prayer and returns the microphone to Mother Spencer.

"My God, my God. Minister, you trying to start something up in here with that prayer? Let me calm myself down. We'll have the scripture reading by First Lady Damita Clark," says Mother Spencer as she rests the microphone on the podium.

"I'll be reading from 1 Thessalonians 5:18. In everything give thanks: for this is the will of God in Christ Jesus concerning you. The Word of the Lord is already blessed." First Lady Damita exits the podium.

"Praise God. You should feel good in your spirit. The praise and worship team is ready, so get into the service with them. God is worthy of all the praise. He woke us up this morning in our right mind and started us on our way. Hallelujah! Don't let this old woman out-dance you."

The organist strikes a key and the anointing in the music provokes a praise from Mother Spencer. Parishioners follow her lead while others scan the crowd. The praise and worship team sing a mix of traditional and contemporary hymns. After praise and worship, Mother Spencer introduces psalmists, rappers, praise dancers, quartets, and choirs. The Holy Spirit takes over the service.

Marcus dances out of his jacket as Precious stands crying with uplifted hands. Layla and Fernando stand holding each other weeping. Tamar and Bryan both get their praise on, dancing out in the aisle. Zion stands clapping his hands, amazed how the Lord still uses his mother. Champagne stands beside Zion, inadvertently putting single ladies on notice. The sound of Mother Spencer's voice makes Champagne want to cut out her eardrums and flush them down the toilet. She looks at her watch, debating if she should leave with the children.

"I'd like to thank everyone for their part in the program. Now it's time for the best part. What time is it?" Mother Spencer asks the crowd.

They respond, "It's time for the Word!"

"It is with great respect I call this man of God to the podium to introduce our honoree. Bishop Clarence Patterson!" proclaims Mother Spencer. The audience gives the bishop a standing ovation.

Bishop Patterson authoritatively stands behind the podium and with a deep, powerful voice says, "God is good all the time."

The congregation responds, "All the time God is good."

"Can we give Mother Spencer a hand praise for the beautiful way she ushered in the Holy Spirit?"

"Yes, she did!"

"She's anointed by God!"

"I love her spirit!" parishioners shout from the pews.

"I won't be before you long. From a child to adulthood, my son has loved the Lord, the people, and anything pertaining to God. He is a third-generation preacher with the anointing of his forefathers' mantle. Things haven't always gone his way, but the songwriter sings troubles don't last always. I contemplate my son is pregnant with a spiritual baby. Right now it's delivery time. Somebody yell, push! Push! I present to some and introduce to others Pastor Demetrius Patterson!"

Father and son embrace onstage. "My father has always been the rock in our family. A godly example of what a man, father, and husband should be in the lives of those he loves. Mother Spencer, it has been a delight to watch the Lord use you. My wife said you were a firecracker. I give honor to God, the ministers, saints, visitors, and friends. If I missed anyone, charge it to my head and not my heart. You can remain seated as I pray. Father God, in the precious name of Jesus, I thank you for each and every soul who had a hand in making today a success. I thank you for all in attendance. I am nothing without you. Let self decrease and spirit man increase. Open your children's ears so they may hear what thus saith the Lord. Amen."

The congregation waits as baby birds to be fed by their mother.

"I'll be reading from Job 13:13-18. My sermon topic is 'You May Know My Storm, but You Don't Know Me.' There are times in our lives when the people in our circle may know of the places you've been, folk you've been with, and errors in your judgment. But I came to let somebody know you are not your mistakes.

"Job's friends knew he was in a dead situation. They thought they knew it was because he sinned against God. The folks in his circle gave him advice from their perspective of his situation. This leads me to conclude that while they may have some of the facts, their perception can still be inaccurate because they are looking through a filtered lens.

"You have to trust God in your dead situation. The scriptures state life and death are in the power of your tongue. Speak life! It is time for the body of Christ to get out of this handicap position. You are waiting for God to move, and He's waiting for you to believe He can do exceedingly, abundantly, above what you can imagine for yourself.

"Let God into your mind to regulate your thoughts. Let Him into your heart to lighten your burdens. Let Him into your home to regulate the atmosphere. Let folks talk! As God gets bigger in your life, their opinions get smaller. Jesus loves you and desires to bless every area of your life. God gives man free will. Will you let Him into your life today? God bless you!" Pastor Patterson ends his sermon and receives a resounding standing ovation from the crowd.

"Thank you, Lord!" "Hallelujah!" "Praise Jesus!"

"Lord, you're worthy!" Parishioners send vocal praises throughout the edifice.

Mother Spencer asks visiting clergy for remarks. Clergy and politicians bestow their congratulatory comments. Pastor Patterson ends the evening's festivities with the benediction, and those in attendance are impressed with the pastor's charismatic delivery of God's Word.

"Pastor did his thing today!" says Bryan.

"Does that mean you would like to join his ministry?" asks Tamar.

"I feel as though we're already members. I love Pastor Patterson. He's a real, straight-up, caring brother. I feel I can learn a lot from him as a man."

"Welcome to our new church!" says Tamar as she embraces Bryan.

"It was a really wonderful service," says Fernando.

"It was an amazing service. I feel as though I have my strength back. I'm glad we came here together. Why are you looking around?" asks Layla.

"I'm looking for Mother Spencer to put my order in for some yeast rolls. I'm hungry."

"We can stop for dinner after we check on Malachi," responds Layla. The Browns leave the sanctuary with a little more than a mustard seed of faith.

"How do you feel about the service?" asks Marcus.

"I'm actually at a loss for words. I always thought people were crazy or possessed, crying, jumping, and dancing all over the church. This is a real man of God. During all my years of going to church with my foster family, I've never experienced what I felt tonight," replies Precious.

"Hold on to Him, and He will hold on to you," says Marcus. He is joyful for Precious' encounter with the Holy Spirit, but he is mindful of who he is dealing with as well.

Champagne peers at the crowd gathered near both entrance and exiting doors. She ponders making a beeline with her children to an alternate side door. Champagne has no time for small talk with Mother Spencer, and she sees Mother Spencer attempting to make her way to her family. Attendees keep interrupting her progress.

Zion waves so that his mother can see him and her grandchildren. "Momma, you were fantastic! Wasn't she, guys? God uses you mightily, Momma."

"Don't you forget it! Where's your wife?" asks Mother Spencer.

"I believe she went to the bathroom. There's probably a long line," Zion responds, covering for his wife.

"Well, babies, I have to go. Please extend my thanks to Champagne."

"Yes ma'am. I love you."

"I love you all, too."

Mother Spencer is whisked away by members of her church to celebrate. Zion and the children are waiting in the SUV for Champagne.

"Sorry for the wait. A few ladies I fellowship with were there. I stopped to chat with them," says Champagne as she buckles her seat belt.

"You knew Momma would want to see you."

"Your mother didn't want to see me."

"Don't you mean you didn't want to see my mother? Never mind; what do you have planned for dinner?" asks Zion.

"Don't worry about it. I always have a plan. You should know that about me by now," Champagne smugly responds, and Zion is oblivious to his wife's indication.

CHAPTER SIXTEEN

Fake Paparazzi

THE CHILDREN AND ZION ARE jubilant to be with Mother Spencer's side of the family. The family has rented the entire amusement park for the day. The children play freely while being supervised by their older cousins. Zion and a few of his cousins take advantage of the mini golf course.

"I can't believe your bougie-ass wife actually allowed you to come and mingle with us commoners. Where is she anyway?" asks cousin Pete.

"She's home sick. I'm a grown-ass man. I come and go as I please," responds Zion.

"I don't know, cousin. If she holds your balls any tighter, you'll end up with a vagina," says cousin Marvin as the men burst into laughter.

"Man, y'all are dogging a brother hard. I may have to go home and lick my wounds," says Zion.

"You can leave if you want to, but Peaches will be here," states Marvin. Zion snaps his neck toward Marvin so quickly it cracks.

"Damn, cuz, aren't you a happily married man? You living the good life," states Pete.

"The grass isn't always greener, and things aren't always as they seem," responds Zion.

His cousin, feeling uncomfortable for him, asks, "Would you like a beer?"

"No, but tell me if Peaches is going to be here today," asks Zion.

"She's in town. You know she loves your mother. I heard she wanted to see some of the family before she left," says Pete.

"Peaches should've been family, but that's ancient history. I heard she married a solid dude," says Marvin.

"Excuse me, fellas. I'm going to check on my children."

"Zion, this is a party. Don't bring your tired-ass baggage out here, depressing the hell out of us. Come back and let me whip your butt in mini golf!" yells Pete as Zion walks away.

Family and friends are still arriving at the amusement park. On his way to see about his children, Zion notices Mother Spencer talking to a beautiful woman. Her physique is familiar. As he gets closer, the breathtaking beauty giggles. Zion has heard that laugh throughout his entire life. He walks briskly toward them.

"It's good to see you, sweetheart. Stay in touch. I love you," says Mother Spencer as she hugs Peaches.

"I love you, too."

Mother Spencer stares firmly at Zion as she walks past him, rubbing his back with her hand and allowing him and Peaches to converse.

"I have so many questions."

"I'm sure you do, Zion, but everything that needed to be said was in my letter."

"Peaches, I'm so sorry for so many things. I messed up. You're the only woman I've ever truly loved and I've lost you. You were never second to me...not in my heart. Why wouldn't you tell me you were married?" inquires Zion.

"What difference would it have made? You continued to pursue me when you did find out. What we shared was beautiful, but it's over. We can't change the past. I'm happily married to a wonderful man, and I don't want to lose him. The decisions we made are final, and we have to live with them," says Peaches as she tries to walk away.

Zion grabs her by the forearm. "Please allow me five more minutes of your time," implores Zion and Peaches obliges. "I don't want to hurt you. I'm sorry for not treating you like the queen you are. Forgive me for being such a fool."

"There's nothing to forgive, Zion. As I told you in the letter, I'll always carry a part of you with me, but now I have to say goodbye, Zion." Zion pulls Peaches close to him and kisses her softly on the lips. She caresses his face and sweeps the tear falling from his eye with her thumb. Then Peaches turns, walks away, and vanishes within the crowd. Zion continues to stand there, hoping this is a nightmare he will awaken from in the morning.

Mother Spencer's guest, Evangelist Mason, has been watching the drama unfold between Zion and Peaches from behind a park dumpster. She has taken numerous pictures of their encounter with her smartphone. Evangelist Mason shakes her head as she reviews the pictures. She selects the most damning ones to implement her evil deed.

Champagne is home alone, enjoying the quiet and a large slice of ice cream cake when her cell phone vibrates on the glass end table. She puts a fork full of cake in her mouth as she picks up her phone with her other hand.

"Evangelist Mason, I don't feel like company," says Champagne as she opens the text message.

"You said you wanted to know no matter what, but I'm sorry to send you this. Please review the following attachments. Again, I'm really sorry. You do deserve better, Champagne," says Evangelist Mason's text.

Champagne's phone then dings repeatedly as Evangelist Mason sends multiple pictures of Zion and Peaches.

"No, no, not that bitch! You're in public with my children!" screams Champagne as she begins smashing vases and mirrors, destroying their family room. "You've always been a thorn in my side! I'll be rid of you. I'm his wife until death do us part," yells Champagne as she glares at the pictures on her smartphone. She comes to herself and hurries to clean up the shattered pottery and glass.

Zion's children and cousins are like peas in a pod. "Adults can learn a lot from children. They're so forgiving and not judgmental," says Mother Spencer as she sits beside Zion on a bench. "How are you, son?"

"You were right, Momma. I was a selfish idiot. I've lost her."

"My dear boy, my heart breaks for you. All I've ever wanted was for you to be happy. Since Peaches has made the decision to remain with her husband, are you going to stay with Champagne?"

"I don't want to, but for the kids I'll stay with her."

"Pray about it. Don't sacrifice your happiness for your children. It won't benefit them in the long run."

"I'm numb. I can't think straight right now, Momma. I'm going to get my kids and head on home."

"I understand. Drive carefully and text me when you get home."

"Yes ma'am," responds Zion as he hugs his mother goodbye. Zion and his children take time to speak to each of their family members before leaving the amusement park.

Once they arrive, the children exuberantly enter their home and begin to tell their mother of all the fun they've had with their cousins. Champagne cuts the children short, instructing them upstairs to shower. She refuses to allow her children on the furniture until they have washed off the stench of those people.

Champagne asks Zion, "How was it, spending time with the children by yourself?"

"I'd hardly say I was alone. We were surrounded by family and friends. The children had such a wonderful time," responds Zion.

"Did you see anyone special today?" inquires Champagne.

"Every person I saw today was special. Family, a few people from my old neighborhood, and church folk were there."

"Who did you see from your old neighborhood?"

"Champagne, you didn't care enough to come, but you felt well enough to redecorate the family room. Stop asking questions about people you care nothing about," firmly responds Zion.

Disgusted by his response, Champagne stomps upstairs to check on the children.

The reality of losing Peaches has finally sunk into Zion's mind and heart. He determines to focus on the characteristics he likes about Champagne, hoping to fall in love with the mother of his children.

Zion removes a picture of Peaches from his wallet. He sits back on the sofa, smiling and recalling how good Peaches felt in his arms. He stares at the picture before tearing it in half and placing it back into his wallet.

Zion hasn't noticed Champagne standing on the landing upstairs, scowling at him. She removes her phone from her pocket to review the images of her husband in the arms of that damn woman.

"I have turned the other cheek more times than I can count. I'll do what I have to do to be rid of you once and for all, bitch. You won't destroy my family," declares Champagne to herself.

CHAPTER SEVENTEEN

Passions Ignite

BRYAN AND TAMAR HAVE BEEN meeting with Pastor Patterson for weekly counseling sessions for the past few months.

"I'm delighted with the progress you both have made individually and together as a happily married couple," states Pastor Patterson.

"I can't tell you how much the Bible-study homework you insisted we incorporate into our daily lives has helped strengthen and empower us," admits Tamar.

"Our marriage is surely on the high road to recovery. Once I was able to see myself as God sees me, I was able to walk in the freedom of His forgiveness. I left the past in the past. That opened the door for me to love Tamar in a way I never thought I'd experience in my lifetime," affirms Bryan.

"Glory be to God. You two make what I do worth it. There's no further need for counseling sessions. Unless an issue arises, you're released to continue to work together as a team without my guidance," says Pastor Patterson. The Deputys stand and hug the pastor, thanking him for his prayers, dedication, and patience with them.

"Tamar, I'd like to speak with the pastor for a moment in private. Man to man. Can you wait for me in the car?"

"Sure," Tamar obliges as she walks out of the pastor's office.

"Is there a problem, Bryan?"

"No sir, quite the opposite. I need your help in executing a monumental surprise celebrating my wife."

"Count me in, Bryan! I love surprises. What do you have in mind?" asks the Pastor, and Bryan details a night his wife will never forget.

On their way home, Tamar asks, "What were you discussing with Pastor Patterson?"

"Men stuff," responds Bryan.

"I hear you, buddy." Tamar enters their home as Bryan purposefully lags behind.

He removes a large rectangular box with a red bow, a medium-sized square box, and a small box from the trunk of his vehicle.

"What's all this?" Tamar asks as Bryan enters with the boxes stacked one on top of the other. He sets the boxes on the loveseat and instructs Tamar to have a seat. Bryan removes the smallest black velvet box from his pocket and gets on one knee. He opens the box, revealing an eighteen-karat white gold, one-carat blue princess-cut diamond ring.

"Tamar, I'm so in love with you. Your love consumed and tamed me. I'll spend the rest of my life making every one of your days better than the day before. You're all I need, so in the presence of God, will you marry me?"

A tearful, speechless Tamar nods her head "yes" as Bryan slides the ring onto her finger. She is mesmerized by the sparkling gem. When they married almost ten years ago, they couldn't afford wedding rings. This ring is a true testament to Bryan's commitment to their marriage and to Christ. His mother would be so proud of him.

"I've been working really hard as a foreman at the company with you as my motivation. Baby, I'm showing off my brown sugar tonight! There's a dress and shoes in the boxes. I hope you like it. Be ready by six o'clock sharp. I'll return shortly. I love you. You've made me the happiest man alive!" Bryan says as he rushes out the door. Tamar is beyond happy as she races upstairs to get ready for an evening with her best friend.

After she showers, Tamar stares in the mirror, pondering how to style her hair. Her go-to style is a bun or ponytail, but tonight's special. Tamar searches the internet for an elegant yet different hair style.

"This is perfect!" she says as she watches the how-to video. It takes a few tries before Tamar successfully completes her new hairdo, and then she accents the fishtail braid with pearls.

With her hair done, Tamar opens the box with the red bow. "Oh my, Bryan must have something really special in store for me tonight," Tamar says aloud as she gazes at the sleeveless, off-white, lace and silk knee-length dress. The nude, ankle-strap mid-heel complements the dress superbly.

Now that she's seen her dress, Tamar decides to embrace her natural facial features. She doesn't want to hide them. She applies neutral shades of makeup to her face, but Bryan loves her full, luscious lips, so Tamar accentuates them with a rich, deep-red lipstick. She dresses carefully, so as not to disturb her makeup and hair.

"You clean up really good, sister girl," Tamar says aloud to herself as she reviews her reflection in the mirror. The hours fly by, and soon it is five o'clock.

Tamar decides to play music while she awaits Bryan's return. She is downstairs dancing to "Go Get It" by Mary Mary when Bryan hurries through the door. The vision of his wife causes him to pause.

"Wow, I may need to call the fire department because you are hot!" yells Bryan.

Tamar blushes and replies, "It's almost six o'clock. You better go get dressed. Do you hear me?"

"Yes, but I have a problem. Look what you made me do."

"What is it?" asks a concerned Tamar. Bryan points downward.

"An erection! Bryan, you are not going to mess up my hair and makeup. You are going to take a shower, so make it do what it do. Put that thing away and save it for later," says a playful Tamar.

"Just heartless." Laughing, Bryan shakes his head as he goes upstairs. Thirty minutes later, Bryan comes downstairs cleaner than the board of health.

He's wearing a black suit with a cream shirt. His tie and matching handkerchief have variations of purple and cream. The couple laugh and dance together in the middle of their living room but are interrupted by a knock at the door. Bryan opens the door.

"Good evening, Pastor Patterson. What can we do for you?" asks Tamar.

"I'm actually here at your husband's request."

Tamar turns her attention to Bryan. "Honey, what's going on?"

"I want to eradicate any doubts that you may have in the back of your mind as to how committed I am to you. I asked Pastor to come by to help us renew our vows. I hope you don't mind," says Bryan.

"I told you not to mess up my makeup," responds a tearful Tamar. "I would love to remarry you."

The pastor enters and stands in front of the fireplace. Tamar stands to the pastor's left and Bryan to his right. Pastor Patterson begins their impromptu vow-renewal ceremony.

"Dear, God. Thank you for your enduring love and for giving the gift of love to Bryan and Tamar. Today they want to rededicate that love to each other. We are grateful that your loving presence will surround this vow-renewal ceremony and be with us now and forever. Amen.

"Hold hands and face each other," the pastor instructs them. "Bryan, begin."

"Tamar, I stand once again before you to renew our vows of marriage. I have shed the old man, and with a renewed mind, heart, and soul I promise to remain strong in my love, gentle in my care, and unwavering in my trust. In the name of our Lord and Savior Jesus Christ, I offer you my heart as my lover, partner, and lifetime companion. You are the chips to my dip. I love you.

"I would not be the man standing here today without your unconditional love. You loved me when I didn't love myself. You saved me when I didn't realize I needed to be saved. The light in your life drew me in and compelled me to want to be more. I could not have asked for a better wife than what God handpicked—especially for an undeserving man as me. I am grateful the Lord favored me to be the man you'd call husband."

Tamar is awestruck and overwhelmed by Bryan's heartfelt vows.

"Bryan, ten years ago I promised to love you in sickness and health, for better or worse, until death do us part. This promise to you was a covenant with God. I choose to forget the things which are behind, and stretch forward to the things which are before us. Yes, our vows have been tested these past few years, but we are on the other side of the mountain. Today is our fresh start. I am delighted to reaffirm my commitment to love, honor, and support you, in sickness and in health, for better or for worse, for as long as we both shall live."

The couple's hands are clasped and Pastor Patterson places his hands over theirs.

"The circle is a symbol of unity and peace. These rings represent an unbroken circle solidifying the vows and promises you've made to each other this day. Bryan and Tamar, I reaffirm you as husband and wife. What God hath joined together, let no man put asunder. You may seal your renewal of marriage vows with a kiss!"

The couple kiss tenderly as their tears flow.

"It is with great honor I present you as Mr. and Mrs. Bryan Deputy," announces Pastor Patterson.

Bryan hugs Tamar tightly and lifts her off her feet.

Joyous laughter fills the room.

"Pastor, you're the man! I appreciate you coming through for a brother. Thank you so much."

"Bryan, this has made my week. I'm so happy for you both. God bless you. I look forward to seeing you at Sunday's service. Enjoy the rest of your evening," Pastor Patterson says as he leaves their home.

Tamar stares at Bryan seductively. "No, Tamar! I have a whole evening planned for us. Let's go now or we won't be leaving at all," Bryan says as he opens the front door and motions for Tamar to exit. "Are you ready to see what else I have in store for you tonight?" asks Bryan as he opens the car door for Tamar.

"I can hardly believe what you've been able to do. What's next?"

"I hope you're hungry. Here...put this on. I want this to be a surprise." Bryan instructs Tamar to place a blindfold over her eyes.

Every few minutes Tamar asks, "Are we there yet?"

Bryan laughs and responds, "No, five more minutes."

Finally, the Deputys have reached their destination, and Tamar removes the blindfold. "Oh baby, I've always wanted to dine here. Bryan, you didn't..."

"This is your night! Don't worry about a thing. I got this and I got you." The valet parks their vehicle as they enter Indulge, a fine-dining establishment specializing in modern interpretations of soul food and Eastern Shore delicacies.

The rich ebony tones from the wooden bar and tables are accented with pops of orange and turquoise. The leather dining chairs with iron accents provide a beautiful contrast against the crisp linen table covers. The natural travertine floors, cream granite, and pillars throughout give the restaurant an elegant appeal. The maître d' is dressed in a black and white suit. The hostesses and wait staff are all dressed in neatly pressed black and white coordinating uniforms.

"Good evening, Mr. and Mrs. Deputy. Please accompany me to your table," instructs a hostess.

The couple sits and Tamar immediately feels overwhelmed by all the formal silverware and dinnerware on the table. The hostess, noticing Tamar's distress, removes the majority of the silverware, leaving a knife, fork, and spoon atop her linen napkin. The hostess nods and smiles at Tamar saying, "Your waiter will be with you shortly. Enjoy your evening."

"Thank you," the couple responds in unison.

"I still can't believe we're here."

"Believe it, baby! This is just the beginning of our new life together," says Bryan. Tamar peruses the menu.

"Everything seems delicious. I don't know what to choose."

Bryan responds, "You haven't had a good crab cake since Mommom Hattie Mae passed away. I'm pretty sure they can satisfy your fix."

"What are you going to order?" asks Tamar.

"You know I love that surf and turf. This fourteen-ounce New York strip that comes with a sixteen-ounce lobster tail is right up my alley."

"Your eyes are bigger than your stomach. I want fried green tomatoes!" says Tamar.

"Whose eyes are bigger than their stomach?" taunts Bryan.

The Deputys place their order with the waitress, and then a little later, a waiter arrives pushing a chrome cart with a silver dome. He removes the dome, and the aroma immediately causes the couple to salivate. The waiter sets the plates of food on the table. He leaves, and they bless the food and savor every delectable bite.

"Eating food this scrumptious has got to be a sin," says Tamar.

"This is the life, baby! I'm about to hurt myself if I take one more bite. Would you like to walk this meal off at the beach?" inquires Bryan.

"No. I'd like to help you with the problem you had earlier this evening," his wife responds enticingly.

"Check, please!" announces Bryan.

He pays for dinner, the valet retrieves their vehicle, and Bryan races home. The vehicle is barely in park when the love-struck couple rushes out toward their front door.

Once inside, Tamar and Bryan leave a trail of shoes, clothing, and undergarments from the front door and up the stairs to the master bedroom.

Tamar pushes Bryan onto the bed and climbs on top of him. They kiss passionately as Bryan fondles Tamar's secret place. Her moans send chills through Bryan's body. They roll around on the bed until Tamar is lying on her back. Bryan places a path of soft kisses from her lips to her belly button. He has now reached his destination— her hot, creamy center. Tamar arches her back, grabbing the sheets and screaming Bryan's name as he devours her. The figure eights he is doing with his tongue around her clitoris cause Tamar to have an F5 orgasm.

Bryan gazes at Tamar with a smile on his face. "Lay on the bed," demands Tamar seductively. Donning a hat, she straddles Bryan, giving him her best reverse cowgirl. He holds on to her hips as she squeezes him tightly, gliding up and down. Bryan removes the pillow from under his head and rips the pillowcase off, throwing them both on the floor.

"What are you doing to me, Tamar? It's so good!"

"I'm putting in work, Poppa! You like that?"

"I love it!" responds Bryan as he commences to smacking Tamar's ass. The couple reaches an epic climax as they moan, scream, and grab for things not there. The couple collapse in bed next to each other.

Panting, Bryan asks, "How did you learn to do that?"

"Kegel Master 2000!" responds Tamar as she chuckles.

"I love you, Tamar. If this is what it feels like to be a happily married man, sign me up for thirty more years."

"I love you more. I hope you're ready for round two!"

CHAPTER EIGHTEEN

The Confrontation

MARCUS ARRIVES HOME FROM WORK to find Precious lying on the sofa. Balled-up tissues overflow from a small plastic bag on the floor near her. A box of cold and flu medicine sits beside a mug on the coffee table. She has a productive, barking cough.

"I see someone isn't feeling well," says Marcus.

"I feel horrible. My plan to search for a new job today has been derailed by this cold," responds Precious.

"Have you eaten today?"

"No. I haven't had the energy to boil water," responds Precious.

Marcus goes into the kitchen, removes chicken thighs from the refrigerator, and prepares them for baking. He sautés onions, fills the pot with water, and adds chicken base and a frozen bag of mixed vegetables. Marcus then goes into the bathroom. He removes the eucalyptus bath salts from the closet and shakes them into the hot water he's been running in the bathtub.

"Precious, come with me, please." She follows Marcus as he leads her into the bathroom. The steam-scented air fills her nostrils.

"After all I've put you through, you still want to take care of me. Thank you," says Precious.

"Enjoy your bath. I'll finish dinner and sanitize out here," says Marcus as he chuckles and closes the door. He cleans and sprays disinfectant throughout the living room. Marcus even tidies up the guest room where Precious has been sleeping for the past few months. The chicken is finished baking, so Marcus shreds the meat from the bone and adds it to the pot with eggs noodles.

"Mmm, she'll enjoy this," he says to himself as he tastes the soup. Then he rummages through the box of DVDs in the den. "Got it!" he says aloud to himself.

"Knock, knock. Precious, dinner is finished. I'll fix you a plate when you come out," says Marcus on the other side of the bathroom door.

"Okay," responds Precious.

She can't help but feel like an idiot as she soaks her aching body. Marcus's kindness toward her compounds the guilt she feels for betraying him. Precious begins to cry uncontrollably as she bathes herself.

"I want to be clean. Wash me whiter than snow. God, I don't want to be like this. I want to change, but I don't know how to do it. Help me, please. If Marcus will have me, help me to be the wife he deserves. God, I'm so sorry. Change me now! In Jesus' name I pray. Amen," prays Precious as she gets out of the tub.

A tray table placed beside the sofa has a hot bowl of soup, a glass of orange juice, and a buttered roll on it. Precious walks into the living room in her pajamas.

"Have a seat and enjoy your meal. Be careful. It's hot. Are you feeling better?" asks Marcus.

"Yes. I'm feeling so much better. Thank you so much. The soup is delicious," says Precious.

"I have a surprise for you," Marcus says as he pushes play on the DVD remote control.

"No, you didn't, Marcus! This is my favorite movie! I haven't seen the 1959 version of *Imitation of Life* in years."

"I thought it'd help cheer you up."

Sitting on the sofa, Precious enjoys her dinner and the company of her husband. She and Marcus haven't spent quality alone time together in months.

"Isn't this your favorite part?" Marcus says as he turns to face Precious.

She has fallen asleep on the sofa. He places a blanket over Precious and watches her as she sleeps.

"I love you so much, but I can't trust you," says Marcus.

"Trust me," says the Holy Spirit. Marcus realizes within himself that God is truly in control of his marriage. He decides to help Precious make a decision about her past. She has considered reaching out to members of her estranged family for years. For weeks now, Marcus has known the address of Precious' mother. The perfect time hasn't presented itself for him to tell her, but tomorrow is the day his wife will learn the truth. Marcus puts the leftover soup away and straightens the house before going to bed himself.

Precious awakens the next morning, feeling mostly back to herself. Her cold symptoms and the soreness in her body are gone, so she fixes Marcus a good ole country breakfast. The smell of cinnamon French toast, bacon, scrapple, scrambled eggs, grits, fried potatoes, and cornbread saturates the air, coaxing Marcus to awaken from his slumber.

"Good morning," says Marcus as he enters the kitchen.

"Good morning. You ruined my surprise. I wanted to bring you breakfast in bed. You took such good care of me yesterday," responds Precious.

"In sickness and in health…I meant those words when I said them."

"For better or for worse...I've been responsible for your worse. I don't know how to fix us. I feel your reluctance to believe me...and why would you? I've lied and reneged on my word countless times. But it's different this time, Marcus. I'm different. I do love you," proclaims Precious.

"I feel your sincerity. I want to help you heal from your past—it's had such a stronghold over your life. It's time to face your past, break free from it, and move forward without the burdens of what tried to destroy you. There's a ministry in your misery. God has given you the tools in His Word. Tap into it and break yourself free!" declares Marcus.

"How do I start?" asks Precious.

"Confront your mother. When you're ready, I'll be there with you. Here's her address," answers Marcus as he slides a sheet of paper across the counter toward Precious.

"I want my new and improved life back today! We're taking a road trip. Ready or not, I'm going to see my mother today."

Marcus and Precious enjoy their delicious breakfast as they sit on the deck. The sun shining on the pond causes the surrounding trees to reflect off the water as a mirror.

"It's so peaceful here," admits Precious. "There's supposed to be peace in your home."

"Is this my home, Marcus?"

"Time will tell," he says.

The Farringtons finish breakfast and prepare themselves for the confrontation between Precious and her mother. They arrive to a splendid waterfront Cape Cod with sculpted landscaping in an affluent neighborhood in Ocean City, Maryland.

"She obviously had the means to take care of me," says Precious.

"Maybe she came into money later in her life," states Marcus optimistically.

"Pray for me."

"I will, Precious."

She knocks on the door. "Just a minute," responds a voice from inside. The door opens, and it's as if Precious is looking into a mirror in the future.

"Are you Beatrice St. John?"

"Yes."

"I am…" Precious is unable to finish her sentence.

"I know who you are. Come in, Precious," says her mother. "Would you like something to drink?" asks Beatrice.

"No, thank you," responds Precious.

"Have a seat," instructs her mother. "What can I do for you? Are you here for money?" asks Beatrice.

"No! I want to know why you gave me away."

"There are doors that should remain locked, Precious. You may not be able to handle what you're walking into."

"I don't want riddles. I want the truth. Why didn't you keep me, Mother?" Precious asks forcefully.

"My husband and I were struggling in Virginia. He started getting sick. When we finally got enough money together to visit the doctor, he was diagnosed with end-stage cancer. The bishop of the church we visited sometimes would bring us food and give us a little money to help with bills. I trusted and confided in him. One evening, when he brought bags of groceries because our cupboards were empty, he asked, 'What are you going to give me?'

"I had no education, my husband was lying in the bed in the next room dying, and my stomach was growling, so I did what I had to do to survive. My husband died and I was pregnant. Rumors spread quickly through a small town. It wasn't long before the bishop's wife was knocking at my door. She gave me one thousand dollars to leave town. So I did.

"We moved around a lot before I decided I couldn't provide for you. You were a constant reminder of that man. I figured I'd give you back to the church.

"You seem to be a beautiful young woman. I see a lovely diamond ring on your finger. You must be married. My decision seems to have worked for the both of us. I remarried a wonderful man who was a good provider in life but a better provider in death," divulges Beatrice.

"Your decision brought a level of pain no child should have to endure. I went through various foster parents, never knowing how long I'd be in that home. I was beaten and sexually abused by the church folks you entrusted to protect me."

"Why would you stay there?" asks Beatrice.

"You're asking adult me why adolescent me didn't leave my abusers? I was a kid! Where was I going to go? What was I going to do? I was afraid and alone. You need to take your part in my dysfunction! I'm sorry that when you look at me you see a disgusting mistake. I'm sorry that you couldn't love me past your own pain. You can get back to your life as if I never existed, but answer one last question. Who is my father?" inquires Precious.

"The late Bishop Clarence Patterson Sr. Will you leave now? I'm expecting company momentarily," says Beatrice.

Precious stands and walks toward the door. She turns to face her mother and scans the exquisitely decorated home.

"I don't hate you, for you gave me life. I really feel sorry for you. I can live without the apology you'll never give me. I'll be praying for you, Mother. I love you. Goodbye," Precious says as she turns and walks out of her mother's life as quickly as she walked into it.

It begins to rain, and a rainbow appears behind the car where Marcus awaits her return. She releases the tears she was holding and begins to thank God for freeing her—freeing her from her past, from her mistakes, and from the opinions of others. Her yes to God has released her from the bondage in her mind.

"How did it go?" asks Marcus.

"I'll tell you all about it. Let's go home," responds Precious.

CHAPTER NINETEEN

Love Is Not Enough

FERNANDO HAS SENT THE NANNY home early to spend the day with his favorite little pal, his son, and the two of them are having a glorious day filled with love and laughter. Fernando and Malachi want to surprise Layla with dinner. She's been working extremely hard to ensure their company maintains their number-one position. The precocious ten-month-old crawls to the front door and hits it with the palms of his hands.

"I see someone is ready to ride. Let's go, buddy," says Fernando as he picks up his son and diaper bag. On their way to the market, Fernando's phone rings.

"Hello."

"What's up, brother? I haven't heard from you in a while. I got some blow that will make you feel like a superhero," says Juney.

"Nah. I'm staying clean for my girl and my son. Do me a favor— lose my number," responds Fernando.

"Is that how you talk to your friends? I'm going to forgive your rudeness and offer you a free sample of the new stash to prove no hard feelings."

"I said no! Don't call me again!" Fernando says as he ends the call.

Juney, though, is not willing to take "no" for an answer from one of his best customers.

"Fellas, find Fernando. When you do, call me. I want to deal with him personally." He sends his flunkies off to do his bidding.

⟋⟍

"I've found him, boss. He's at the market."

"I'm on my way."

Fernando exits the market, pushing Malachi in a cart full of groceries. A candy, green-apple pearl Escalade with blackout rims parks in the crosswalk, blocking Fernando's ability to get to his vehicle. A medium-build, brown-skinned man standing five-feet-eight and wearing a striped shirt, shorts, and loafers steps out of the truck.

"My favorite entrepreneur, I see you on your daddy daycare flow. I respect that. Here's a little appreciation gift," Juney says as he stuffs a baggie into Fernando's pocket. "You enjoy the rest of your day with your son," says Juney as he leaves the market parking lot.

To avoid a confrontation in the presence of his son, Fernando says nothing. He hurries to put his son and the groceries in the car.

"The traffic's starting to get bad, little man," Fernando says as he monitors his son from the rearview mirror. "Come on! I don't want to miss my exit. These damn cars must know I have plans. We'll be home in ten minutes, Malachi," says Fernando.

"Finally." Fernando sees a clear path. His signal light flashes as he begins to merge into the lane. He smiles as he checks the rearview mirror again and sees Malachi falling asleep.

Boom!

Fernando is knocked unconscious when the air bag smashes into his head.

◡

Layla is on her way home and wondering if she has been too hard on Fernando.

"My goodness. What's happened up there?" she says aloud to herself as ambulances pass her in the opposite lane. Her phone begins to ring.

"Hello."

"Layla, it's Lavarius. There's been an accident. I need you to get to the hospital. Are you able to drive? If not, I'll come get you."

"Yes. I'm driving now. I'll see you shortly." She turns her hazard lights on and rides the shoulder at times to take the exit straight to the hospital. Layla hastily parks her car and then runs into the hospital.

Lavarius hears her speaking to an attendant and comes to comfort her from the waiting room.

"What's happened? What's going on? Where's my baby?" Layla asks Lavarius.

"A concrete truck slammed into Fernando's truck. He has a few broken ribs, whiplash, and contusions. He's going to be admitted for the night. They're taking him to a room in a couple hours. Malachi was thrown from his car seat into the windshield," says Lavarius.

"What about my baby? How is my baby? I want to see him!" screams Layla.

"Layla Brown," calls a nurse, and Lavarius follows them into a conference room accompanied by a doctor.

"Mrs. Brown, my name is Dr. Johnson, and I've been treating your son. Malachi suffered severe head trauma and had many broken bones. Those injuries, along with internal bleeding, caused him to pass away during surgery. We were unable to revive him. I am so sorry for your loss, ma'am. I'll send a grief counselor to speak with you both."

"Thank you, doctor, for all you've done," says Lavarius. The nurse and doctor leave the room. Layla runs outside and Lavarius chases her. She stops in the middle of the parking lot, falls to her knees, and screams repeatedly. Her father-in-law kneels down next to her and embraces her tightly.

"Hold on, Layla, hold on. We'll get through this together."

"It hurts. It hurts so bad. Why my son?" cries Layla.

"There are times in life when there is no answer to 'Why?' I'm here for you and Fernando for as long as you need me. Baby girl, we have to tell Fernando."

Lavarius' words help strengthen Layla enough to walk back into the hospital. Lavarius asks Layla to go with him to the chapel before seeing Fernando, and they take a seat on a pew.

"I can't even pray right now. When I think things are getting better, another tragedy happens," says Layla.

"If you don't know how to pray, just moan. The Lord understands you," responds Lavarius. After a few minutes, Lavarius says, "Let's go tell Fernando."

Fernando is lying in bed with an IV in his hand, wearing a hospital gown and a neck brace. Both of his eyes are swollen with a lot of bruising around them.

"Hello, son."

"Hey, Dad. Where's Malachi?" Lavarius looks at Layla. "Oh hi, beautiful. I'll be okay. All I need is my little guy. Can you bring him to me?" Fernando asks Layla.

"Fernando, Malachi was hurt pretty bad. The doctors did all they could to save him. He died during surgery," Layla says as she begins to weep.

"No, no, you're wrong! He's in the next room. Tell me he's in the next room! We were almost home. Malachi! Malachi!" Fernando begins to scream and nurses run into the room.

"This will help you relax, Mr. Brown," says a nurse as she injects Ativan into his IV.

"It's my fault. I thought I pushed his buckle in all the way. I'm sorry. God, I'm sorry. Take me instead!" Fernando cries and his father hugs him.

"Get some rest, son. I'll check on you later," Lavarius says as he leaves the room.

Layla sits on the bed with Fernando. "It was an accident. Your vehicle was hit by a concrete truck."

"Can you hand me my jacket?" asks Fernando. Layla hands it to him. "I love you, but you need to leave now," says Fernando.

"What! You want me to leave? Why? What's in your jacket?" Layla attempts to snatch the jacket from Fernando, but he removes the baggie from his pocket before letting it go.

She throws the jacket on the chair and removes the sheet that covers him. "Dope! We lost our son and you want dope! Give it to me! What do you want—me or the baggie?"

"I love you, but I need to forget, even if it's temporary."

"This time love is not enough. Goodbye, Fernando." Layla walks out of Fernando's life forever.

CHAPTER TWENTY

Crossed Paths

PASTOR DEMETRIUS AND FIRST LADY Patterson, along with their daughter Sahara, are preparing themselves for morning service. First Lady is proud of her hardworking husband. Their phone has been ringing off the hook with people wanting him for speaking engagements since the powerfully motivating sermon he preached for the grand celebration.

First Lady has undertaken the daunting task of pressing out Sahara's hair. She is pressing a few strands of hair near the nape of Sahara's neck when the rambunctious daddy's girl runs to him to escape the flat iron.

"My hair is pretty being it, daddy?"

"It's beautiful!"

"Can you tell Mommy I'm done? I want to sit with you and eat my breakfast."

Pastor Patterson is a strong, captivating man, but Sahara turns him into a powderpuff. "Let's go talk to Mommy," says Pastor Patterson.

He walks into their master bedroom where his wife is packing an extra pair of shoes for church. Sahara follows closely behind him. Pastor Patterson winks at his wife. She smiles, asking, "How can I help the two of you?"

"Tell her! Tell her!" shouts Sahara.

"I think Sahara's hair is beautiful the way it is, and we would like you to join us for breakfast."

"Is that true, Sahara?"

"Yes ma'am."

"Turn around so I can inspect this hair of yours." Sahara does as her mother requests. "I'll agree with you and your father this time. Let's have breakfast," says First Lady. The family delights in the times they spend together.

First Lady never had a relationship with her father, and Pastor Patterson has given her the family she has always dreamt of.

"The reason parishioners leave their homes every Sunday is because they have an expectation. They want to encounter God through His holy Word. Let's go and lift the name of Jesus." The Patterson's are on their way to the United Church of Pentecost and Deliverance.

Impressed by Pastor Patterson's transparency, Zion decides to attend Sunday morning service. It's been years since Zion attended a church service outside a holiday or special event. "Champagne, I'm going to visit that new ministry again."

"I'll come with you. Children, get dressed! We're going to church with your father this morning," Champagne says loudly through the house.

"I thought you were going to your church today. Aren't you on the ministerial staff there?" asks Zion.

"Yes, but they can manage without me for one Sunday."

"There's one day a week you're required to show up, and you're calling out. That's not good, Champagne."

The Spencers finish grooming themselves and make their way to the house of the Lord.

~

The fifteen-hundred-seat sanctuary is three-fourths full of congregants—quite a feat for a ten o'clock service. Parishioners are ushered into the presence of the Lord by spiritual dancers with ribbons and a praise team that sings well enough to make an album. A sizable crowd of late parishioners gathers inside the vestibule, waiting to be seated by ushers.

Bryan and Tamar are standing near the large glass entry doors as Marcus and Precious enter. The couples haven't seen each other in months. Precious decides to cut the tension and asks, "Tamar, may I speak with you, please?"

"Good. That will give me a chance to speak with Marcus," responds Bryan.

Tamar stands facing Precious, glaring into her eyes. "Tamar, I wasn't a good friend to you. As a matter of fact, I was a horrible friend. I betrayed your trust and confidence in me. You loved me as a sister, and I hurt you in the worst way. I'm saved now. There's no way I can right my wrongs against you, but I want you to know I'm truly sorry for the pain I caused you. Can you forgive me?" asks Precious.

"You're right. I did love you as my sister. The scar on my heart from your betrayal has healed by the grace of God. I forgive you, but we can never be friends again. I pray for Marcus' sake you're being honest," says Tamar as she walks off into the bathroom.

"Marcus, we were boys for many years. I messed up. It's not a day that goes by that I don't regret what I did to you. I'm sorry, man. I'm so sorry," Bryan tearfully admits.

Marcus hugs Bryan. "I forgive you, I forgive you, I forgive you. Be free from this," commands Marcus. The women rejoin their husbands. "Bryan, do you understand the reason I said 'I forgive you' three times?"

"No."

"Each time represented the Father, the Son, and the Holy Spirit. That seals it!" proclaims Marcus.

"I hear you, minister, and thank you!" says Bryan as he and Tamar are escorted by an usher to their seats. Marcus and Precious are ushered to the opposite side of the edifice.

Pastor Patterson stands at the podium. "A relationship with Jesus Christ is a lifestyle, not something you check off your Sunday to-do list. How do you feel about the people in your life who only call you when they want something? A ride, money, to do a favor? You aren't motivated to help them because they have not invested any of their time into you. We all have someone in our lives that we think of immediately. Think about that person. Think about how it makes you feel.

"Now imagine you are God. How you feel about that person is how God feels when we come to Him with our hand out, like God's a genie in a bottle that's at our beck and call. We got it twisted. God doesn't need us. We need God!

"The Bible is the blueprint for how we should live our lives. Read it. Meditate on the Word. Hebrews 4:12 'For the word of God is quick, and powerful, and sharper than any two-edged sword, piercing even to the dividing asunder of soul and spirit, and of the joints and marrow, and is a discerner of the thoughts and intents of the heart.'

"You may lie to your spouse, your children, your employer, your friends, and even yourself. But you cannot lie to or fool God. Allow Him to lead and guide you in every area of your life. God bless you." Pastor Patterson ends his sermon, and the saints give him a resounding applause.

"I'd like to have a few words before the benediction. I want to thank you all for your support of this ministry. We're new to the area, but not to doing the Lord's work. My family and I would like to greet you as you leave today. Please be patient and keep a uniformed line."

Zion has to shake the pastor's hand, so Champagne reluctantly stands in line with Zion while the children wait in the SUV. Zion finally makes it to the front of the line where Pastor Patterson stands with an open hand and a smile on his face. First Lady's large hat shields the sun from her face. She briefly puts her head down to place a mint in her mouth.

Zion blurts, "Pastor, you're fantastic! I..." First Lady lifts her head up.

"Peaches!" shouts Zion.

"Dominique," Champagne says nastily.

"How do you know my mommy?" asks Sahara. Their attention is immediately drawn to the most gorgeous little blue-eyed girl.

"We used to go to the same school," responds Zion. "What's your name, sir?"

"My name is Zion. What's your name?"

"My name is Sahara. My mommy said I'm named after a dry place."

Zion laughs, saying, "You're smart and beautiful."

Champagne is giving First Lady Dominique Rothschild-Patterson and Sahara evil eyes. First Lady is dumbstruck.

"You fine folks have a blessed day and thank you for coming. I'm sorry, but we have to go now. We look forward to seeing you all next

Sunday. God bless you," says Pastor Patterson as he whisks his family into their BMW X5.

Zion's thoughts are racing when Champagne asks, "Are we going to discuss what just happened?"

"No, we aren't. I'm not having this conversation in front of the children," Zion says, walking quickly and getting into the truck.

"You don't have to, but I will," Champagne replies as she gets into the passenger side of the truck. "Is that your daughter? Is she?" screams Champagne.

Her relentless questioning causes Zion to erupt. "I don't know! Now shut the hell up or get the hell out of my truck!" yells Zion. His response puts the fear of God in the children and Champagne. Everyone is silent for the remaining trip home.

Zion is feeling too many emotions at once. He tells himself, *Peaches would never keep me away from my child. Sahara has such a sunny personality—our bright, charming little daughter. Dominique, you owe me answers and I will get them.*

CHAPTER TWENTY-ONE

Revelations

EMETRIUS ARRIVES HOME WITH HIS FAMILY…and a lot of questions for Dominique. The Patterson's remain downstairs to ensure Sahara isn't privy to their conversation; the little girl has gone to her room to eat a snack and watch TV.

"Is the man we saw today Sahara's biological father?" asks Demetrius.

"Yes," answers Dominique.

"I thought he was dead. Did you tell him about Sahara?"

"No."

"I've never pressured you about her natural father, but I need to know what I'm dealing with. Who is he?" asks Demetrius.

"His name is Zion Spencer. We were childhood sweethearts. Our plan was to get married after college. He married another woman. He felt he made a mistake marrying her. When he went to tell her he was leaving, she was pregnant. I told him to stay with her," confides Dominique.

"And you continued to be with him?" asks Demetrius.

"Yes."

"Have you been with him since we've been married?"

"I told him I was happily married, and I couldn't be the one he turned to anymore."

"Have you had sex with him since we've been married?" Demetrius asks in a raised, bass-filled voice.

"Yes. Once. But I told him it could never happen again. Demetrius, I love you! I want you and only you. You're the best man I've ever known. You're the only father Sahara has known. Please, please don't leave me!" Dominique attempts to hold Demetrius, but he pushes her away.

Dominique sits on the sofa sobbing as Demetrius walks outside. She goes upstairs to check on Sahara, who has fallen asleep with the Gogurt wrapper in her hand. Dominique turns the TV off, pulls a throw over Sahara, and goes back downstairs. She gazes outside at her husband, who is on his knees under their massive yellow poplar tree. Needless to say, he is praying to God.

"Lord, please keep my family together," prays Dominique as she begins to prepare dinner.

⟡

Two hours pass, and Sahara hops down the steps. "Mommy, where's Daddy?"

"He's outside, baby. Don't bother him."

"Okay. I'm hungry. Is the food ready?" asks Sahara.

"Yes, it is," responds Dominique.

Demetrius enters their home, his eyes red and puffy from crying.

"Daddy, were you talking to Jesus?"

"Yes, I was."

"Did you tell Him I said hi from the last time?"

Demetrius chuckles as he holds back tears. "Of course I did."

"You're the best daddy ever!" Sahara says as she leaps into her father's arms.

Demetrius holds her tightly. "Okay, princess, I'm going to take a shower. Then we'll have dinner together as a family. I love you," says Demetrius.

"I love you, too, Daddy."

Dominique wipes the tears from her eyes, discerning her prayers have been answered. Her husband, by the mercy of God, is staying committed to their family.

Demetrius walks past Dominique, and she softly says, "Thank you."

Demetrius looks steadily into Dominique's eyes and points upward as he goes upstairs.

⟨⟩

After his shower, Dominique fixes the family's plates. When they have finished eating, Demetrius removes them from the table saying, "We're going to do something different tonight. Let's watch TV in the family room. My favorite movie as a child is about to come on."

"What movie is that?" asks Sahara.

"*The Wiz!* It's an old movie, but it's really cool. They have costumes, singing, and funny characters," responds Demetrius.

"Mommy, come on!"

"I'm coming," replies Dominique.

They laugh, have pillow fights, and relish each other's company.

"Little miss, it's time for your bath," says Dominique. "But Mommy, I want to watch *The Wiz* again! You can't win…" Sahara sings as her parents laugh.

"You can't win tonight. Do as your mother says, love bug. I'll read you a story before bed."

"All right, Daddy."

"Get your pajamas. I'll be up shortly," says Dominique. Sahara skips up the steps to her bedroom singing, "Ease on down, ease on down the road!"

"She is something else," says Demetrius. Dominique is in the kitchen wiping off the counter. "Come and sit next to me. We need to clear the air."

Dominique does as her husband asks her. "I love you and our little girl more than life itself. I forgive you, but you've broken my trust. We have to set ground rules. There will be no secret meetings or phone calls with Zion. If he wants to be a part of Sahara's life, I need to be included in all decisions. I don't doubt your love for me. What I don't trust is your compulsion to be with your ex. As long as you keep being honest with me about everything, we'll be fine. That's all I need to remain in this marriage. Can you do that for me?" asks Demetrius.

"Yes, yes, I can do anything for you! You've given me so much. No one is worth losing you! I love you, baby," says Dominique, passionately kissing her husband.

"You're not playing fair," says Demetrius.

"It's all or nothing and you have all of me. It's bedtime, but I'm not sleepy," replies Dominique.

"Get our daughter squared away. I'll be waiting for you."

Dominique helps bathe and dress Sahara for bedtime. Demetrius reads her a story as she gets comfy in her bed.

Dominique showers and applies a peach moisturizing soufflé to her body. Her husband enters their bedroom to find his wife lying across the bed wearing a lavender and lace teddy. The peach-scented candles burning throughout the room help intensify the sweet smell of her skin. Demetrius is still upset with his wife, but he cannot resist Peaches. She lures him onto the bed, and the two kiss fervently as they urgently remove each other's garments.

Dominique sucks on his bottom lip, looks into his eyes, and says, "I want you."

"I want you more," replies Demetrius.

"Take me," Dominique whispers in his ear as she licks his lobe with the tip of her tongue.

The love they are making feels like the first time for Dominique. The weight of her secrets fades away as smoke in the wind. Her newfound liberty causes every cell of her body to connect with her husband, a feeling like nothing else Dominique has ever experienced. She submits to the powerful force overtaking her mind and body. Dominique clutches at Demetrius' body as elation penetrates her heart. She is crying and trembling as he holds her in his arms.

"Did I hurt you?" asks Demetrius.

"No."

"What's wrong, darling? Why are you crying?"

"I'm happy. You make me so happy," responds Dominique as she nestles her head on her husband's chest and falls asleep.

CHAPTER TWENTY-TWO

Lose To Win

I T HAS BEEN A FEW DAYS, and Champagne is still seething from the possibility that Zion may have fathered a child with Dominique. Evangelist Mason calls an emergency meeting at her home with local clergy to help Champagne through this tough time.

"Ladies, thank you for coming on such short notice. Our sister in Christ needs to pull from our strength at this time. How are you handling the situation?" asks Evangelist Mason.

"I'm taking it one day at a time. Pastor Patterson doesn't know the woman he's married to like I do. She's a home-wrecking whore! He probably never thought his child could be another man's—my husband's! Mother Spencer presided over their service knowing all this and never said a word. She's always given Zion a free pass concerning how he treats me. What kind of woman of God upholds her son in his wrong? I've never heard her once tell him to be faithful or to love his wife," declares Champagne.

"I was speechless when I saw him with her. Mother Spencer was there. She even spoke with First Lady Patterson before her son did. She gave them alone time. It was a despicable sight to witness. I'm glad I was there to capture the sinful encounter," reveals Evangelist Mason.

Champagne nods her head, encouraging Evangelist Mason to expose the images to the ladies that she captured on her phone.

"Awful!" "Deplorable!" "Shameful!" "A disgrace before God!" are the comments being made in reference to the photos.

"What are you going to do, Champagne?" asks Minister Collins.

First Lady Thomas adds, "You could probably get half of everything in a divorce with these pictures as evidence."

"I'm not leaving Zion. The problem is Dominique. She seduces him. If she crawls back under the rock she came from my marriage could survive this. Dominique, my mother-in-law, and her bastard daughter need to drop off the face of the Earth," admits Champagne.

The ladies scan the room, gathering reactions. They gaze at Champagne and wonder why she holds onto a man that repeatedly disrespects her. The ladies shift the conversation to the upcoming events in their respective ministries as they have lunch.

Champagne doesn't care what anyone thinks about her remaining married to Zion. That's her husband! He may do his dirt, but he always comes back to her. That reason alone gives Champagne a false sense of hope.

⤸

Zion sits at his desk, dazed and confused, unable to focus on work at all. He knows in his heart that the beautiful, curly-haired, blue-eyed girl is his daughter. A DNA test would confirm his suspicions. The gut-wrenching pain of conceding Dominique is married is compounded by the years he has missed with his daughter. Zion cannot turn his back on his child.

He searches the internet for the church website then clicks on the announcements tab for upcoming events.

"Friday Night Fire service starts at seven p.m. I'll be there," says Zion as he reads the announcement aloud. He completes imperative tasks before leaving for the United Church of Pentecost and Deliverance.

Demetrius and Dominique have enjoyed multiple rounds of orgasmic lovemaking throughout the day.

"We'll be late to service if you don't allow me to get dressed. Duty calls."

"My body is calling you," replies Dominique.

"I've answered it numerous times between last night and today. You have twenty minutes to be ready. Is Sahara dressed for service?" asks Demetrius.

"Way to go on killing my mood," jokes Dominique. "I'll check to see if she's gotten dressed yet." She exits the master bedroom, grateful to God for her family.

The Patterson's rush out the door, hoping to make it to church on time. They enter the sanctuary with ten minutes to spare. Pastor

Patterson is ushered to the pulpit. First Lady Dominique Patterson and Sahara are seated on the front row. The service begins, and Pastor motions to his wife that he'd like something to drink. Sahara and her mother enter the pastor's study to retrieve his drink.

Zion parks his car in the adjacent parking lot and enters the church as First Lady Dominique and Sahara exit the pastor's study.

"Peaches!" calls Zion. She turns toward him.

"Mommy, it's Mr. Zion."

To him, the little girl says, "You're late."

Zion smiles then responds, "Yes, I am. Aren't you inquisitive?"

"Mommy, what does 'inquisitive' mean?"

"I'll tell you later. Say bye to Mr. Zion. Take this to your dad and follow the usher," says First Lady as she hands Sahara Pastor's drink. Sahara waves bye to Zion, and he waves back.

First Lady waits until Sahara is out of earshot before asking Zion, "What are you doing here?"

"Peaches, we have unfinished business to discuss."

"We have nothing to discuss. I'm happily married. I'm sorry you are not, but that's not my problem. This isn't the appropriate time or place for this conversation," says First Lady Patterson.

"Fine. You're happily married. Where was all this dutiful-wife routine when you were banging my brains out?"

"I can't do this!" responds First Lady.

"I have one question. Is Sahara my daughter?" asks Zion.

Champagne is on her way home from Evangelist Mason's meeting and decides to ride past the United Church of Pentecost and Deliverance. The breath almost leaves her body when she sees Zion's Tesla in the parking lot across the street. She parks her vehicle in the minister's parking section.

"This ends tonight!" declares Champagne as she removes the Glock she purchased a few weeks ago off the internet. She puts the gun inside her purse, walks briskly toward the church, and bursts into the vestibule where Zion and First Lady have been talking.

Distraught, Champagne stands and stares at the image of her husband alone with her nemesis.

"I have to go. Go home with your wife," says Dominique as she begins walking inside the sanctuary.

"Peaches, answer me!" Zion yells so loudly that a few congregants turn, hearing his voice.

"Yes! You are her biological father. But she has a daddy who loves her. Zion, please, I beg you…go home with your wife." Dominique turns to walk away, but Zion grabs her by the hand.

"That's our daughter. You can't expect me to not be a part of her life. I would've been there for you both. Why?" asks Zion with tears in his eyes.

Champagne is crying and shaking her head. She removes the gun from her purse, screaming, "No! No! You can't have him!"

Parishioners notice the gun and call the police. Pastor Patterson is advised there's a gunman in the sanctuary, and he begins to frantically search for Sahara and his wife. He instructs the ministers and ushers to get churchgoers out of the building.

"Daddy! Daddy!" calls Sahara as she is lost in the chaos.

"I hear you, baby! I'm coming for you!" says Pastor Patterson as he runs to the back of the church near the vestibule.

Zion uses his body to shield Peaches from the range of his wife's gun. "What are you doing, Champagne?" asks Zion.

155

"Do you think all the years I've spent planning to be a part of your life are going to end with you leaving me? Hell no! Dominique and your bastard daughter will always be a factor in your life. They need to be erased forever!" proclaims Champagne.

"I'll come home with you. Just put the gun down," says Zion.

"No! It's too late for that. I've been living in the shadow of your beloved Peaches our entire marriage. She has to die! It's the only way!"

Champagne fires the gun and Dominique screams, but the bullet misses her.

Frightened by the sound of the gunfire, Sahara starts to cry, "Mommy! Daddy! Where are you?"

"I see a more suitable target," laughs Champagne as she aims her gun toward Sahara.

"No, God, please! Get down, baby!" screams Dominique.

Pastor Patterson sees the gun and Sahara, who is a few feet away. He leaps over chairs, trying to get to his daughter, who is unaware of the danger she is in.

Champagne fires another shot and Zion tackles her to the floor. They wrestle for the gun, and Zion manages to get his hand on it but Champagne will not release her grasp on the gun. It discharges another round.

"Zion!" screams Dominique.

Champagne smiles, saying, "I just wanted you to love me. Why did you do this to me?"

"Why did you let me?" asks Zion.

Champagne closes her eyes and dies. Zion rises from the floor, covered in Champagne's blood. He and Dominique run toward the sanctuary where Pastor Patterson is holding an unconscious and wounded Sahara.

Paramedics rush into the church and place Sahara onto a stretcher.

Pastor Patterson embraces Dominique tightly as he kisses her and then he shakes Zion's hand. "Thank you for protecting my family. You two ride in the ambulance with Sahara. I'll stay here to speak with the police. I'll meet you at the hospital as soon as I can. I love you," says Pastor Patterson to his wife.

"I love you, too," she responds.

Pastor Patterson prays as he watches the ambulances until it is out of view.

A hospital attendant escorts Zion and Peaches to a waiting room while Sahara is rushed to the operating room. Her parents pace the floor, awaiting word of her condition.

Pastor Patterson storms into the hospital. A nurse, seeing his distress, assists him and takes him to his wife.

"How is baby girl?" he asks as he enters the waiting area.

Dominique stands to greet him, replying, "I don't know. She's in surgery."

"Are you the parents of Sahara Patterson?" asks the doctor.

Zion, Dominique, and Demetrius say in unison, "Yes."

"How is our daughter?" asks Dominique.

"Your daughter is a lucky young lady. The bullet was one milli-meter away from her brachial artery. If that had been hit, she would have bled to death. We were able to remove the bullet, and she should make a full recovery. With physical therapy, she should regain full range of motion of her arm. We'll closely monitor her over the next twenty-four hours. A nurse will escort you to her room once she's settled in," says the doctor before he leaves the parents to rejoice.

"Zion, this is not the time or place, but once Sahara is well, the three of us need to have a conversation. I'm so very sorry for your loss. Is there anyone we can call for you?" asks Demetrius.

Zion's adrenaline has departed and the gravity of the pastor's condolences brings the reality of Champagne's death. Zion begins to weep for her and his children.

Dominique calls Zion's mother. "Hello, Mother Spencer."

"Dominque, what's going on? I heard about the shooting. Are you okay?"

"Yes ma'am. We're at the hospital. Champagne shot Sahara, but she's on her way to the recovery room. She and Zion were wrestling for her gun when it went off. Champagne's dead. Zion's a mess. Can you gather the family to come get him? He needs you all more than ever," admits Dominique.

"We're on our way!" responds Mother Spencer.

As she ends her call, a nurse comes to greet them. "Sahara is able to have visitors. Follow me."

Zion gathers his composure as Dominique extends her hand for him to come with her and Demetrius.

Sahara lies in bed with wires connected to her, and machines beep around her, monitoring her vital signs. "Daddy, my boo-boo hurts."

"I'll tell the nurse so she can give you some medicine," replies Demetrius.

"Mommy, I was brave. Your friend was brave, too. I saw him stand in front of you when that lady had the gun. I'm sleepy," says Sahara.

"I love you, pumpkin," says her mother.

"You're such a precious little girl. Get some rest. I'll see you later," says Zion as he kisses Sahara on her cheek.

She turns to her side and falls asleep. Her parents watch happily as she snoozes peacefully.

A nurse interrupts their visit, saying, "Excuse me. There are family members in the waiting room asking to speak with a Zion Spencer."

"They're for me. Can you call me if anything changes with Sahara?" asks Zion.

"Sure," replies Dominique.

Zion follows the nurse to greet his family in the waiting room. When he sees Mother Spencer, he collapses in her arms and weeps inconsolably. His family surrounds him.

∾

A few days after Champagne's death, her family takes possession of her body and excludes Zion from the funeral arrangements—they blame Zion for her erratic and uncharacteristic behavior.

They hold her funeral at an opulent, historic Catholic church. Clergy, business associates of Zion and her father, and friends and family from across the United States come to pay their final respects to Champagne Carter-Spencer.

Zion, his children, and Mother Spencer enter the sanctuary. "You actually have the audacity to show your face here. Your philandering ways pushed Champagne over the edge. Everyone knows it. If it weren't for her children, your black ass wouldn't be allowed to set foot in here today. It should be you in that casket instead of my baby!" proclaims Mrs. Carter.

Zion is too numb to respond to Champagne's mother. "You people with your big mouths, big I's and little U's, big houses, big egos, and clout never taught your daughter that love is not for sale! If you put as much substance as you did status into your daughter's mental well-being, maybe she would be here today. Champagne was responsible for her own actions. He's grieving, too, so back off of my boy. Mr. Carter, I suggest you take your wife outside to get some fresh air. We'll seat ourselves," responds Mother Spencer.

The funeral is short, yet Mrs. Carter has to be removed from the church numerous times during the service. Champagne's children kiss their mother before the casket is closed and ushered out of the sanctuary. Their tears break Mother Spencer's heart as she attempts to help Zion console them.

Once they leave the burial site, Zion decides they will not accompany the remaining guests to the repast. He and Mother Spencer spend a quiet evening at home with the children. When they're upstairs changing into their pajamas and Mother Spencer is preparing an early dinner, Zion asks, "Momma, can you move in to help me with the kids? It'll be temporary, but I feel they need a sense of normalcy."

"I'd do anything to help my grandbabies."

"Speaking of grandchildren, Sahara is your granddaughter," admits Zion.

Mother Spencer takes a deep breath, exhales, and responds, "I thought so, but it wasn't my place to mention it. I knew when I looked into those beautiful blue eyes she was my granddaughter. That's a rare trait. Pastor Patterson loves her dearly. You couldn't ask for a better man to raise your daughter."

"I want to be a part of her life, Momma. Is that too much to ask?"

"No, but focus on the children you have under the same roof as you. They need you now more than ever. Their lives will never be the same. Sahara's life is back to normal. Everyone in this situation needs time to heal," says Mother Gayle.

The children rejoin their father and grandmother in the kitchen and help her prepare dinner. Zion shares fond memories with the children of their mother as they view photo albums. He tucks each of the children into bed and kisses them goodnight.

Dominique and Demetrius, with frequent visits from Zion, have nursed Sahara back to her healthy self. During her six-week checkup, she is given a clean bill of health.

Dominique enters Sahara's bedroom, asking, "Are you hungry? I've fixed a yummy breakfast."

"I'm hungry, thirsty, and my boo-boo itches," says Sahara as she scratches at her wound.

"Don't do that! Oh, I'll put some vitamin E oil on it. It's probably dry," responds Dominique. The two walk downstairs holding hands.

"Good morning, princess. How are you feeling today?" asks Demetrius.

"I'm good. Can I watch cartoons?"

"Yes, but only for an hour," replies her father. Her parents observe her as she devours breakfast.

"God is so good. We could have lost our baby," says Demetrius.

"I'm grateful to Him every day," replies Dominique. "Once the sitter arrives, I feel today is a good day to have Zion come over to meet with us. He's been an instrumental part of Sahara's healing process. However, we all need to know where he stands."

Demetrius calls Zion. "Good morning, Zion. How are you?"

"Today's a good day. Is everything all right with Sahara?"

"Yes. She's great. Her mother and I wanted to know if you'd be able to meet with us today? We'd like to discuss our roles in Sahara's life. Are you up for this conversation?"

"Sure."

"Can you meet us at our home around one o'clock?"

"Yes," responds Zion.

"We'll see you then," replies Demetrius, and then he ends the call. To Dominique he says, "He's agreed to meet with us this afternoon."

"This should be very interesting," responds Dominique.

"All we can do is pray and hope for the best," replies Demetrius as he enters his office to prepare for Zion's arrival.

Dominique isn't a pessimist, but her familiarity with Zion's passion for what he wants makes her reluctant to believe in an agreeable outcome.

Zion arrives promptly, and Demetrius escorts him to his office. Dominique is sitting at the conference table as the men enter. Demetrius instructs Zion to sit across from him and his wife.

"Zion, we'd like to thank you for coming on such short notice. How are you and your children doing since the passing of your wife?" asks Demetrius.

"We've been managing, making daily strides. It's been a blessing having my mother live with us."

"That's good news. We'd like to understand your intentions concerning Sahara," states Demetrius.

"I'm not here to disrupt her life. I'd like to get to know her. I can't get back the years I've lost, but I refuse to lose another day. I want her to know I love her. You realize how important family is to me. Why would you keep me from my child, Dominique?" asks Zion.

"You would have relinquished everything to be with us. You've worked too hard, and I didn't want to become your burden. I could never live my life knowing I took you away from your children. I sure as hell didn't feel comfortable with co-parenting. Champagne confirmed my fears as to how she'd treat my daughter. I wanted Sahara to have a life filled with love, kindness, and compassion without drama. Demetrius has given her that and so much more.

"I want her to know you're her biological father, but not yet. Sahara's too young to understand this. She's still recuperating from being shot. I think it's best for now that there are no new life-changing events. We'll allow you ample opportunities to spend time with Sahara. I'm pretty sure Mother Spencer would welcome the opportunity to spend time with her granddaughter. Our main objective is to keep her safe," responds Dominique.

"I'll agree to her not being told I'm her father for now. I have and will continue to protect her. I'm not the bad guy. I'll call first before stopping by and schedule play dates that coincide with your schedules. If I feel any opposition, I'll assert my rights as her father," states Zion.

"I believed I was making the best decision for her. Honestly, I didn't want to complicate your life. I'm sorry, Zion. Can you forgive me?"

"Dominique, I can't say you were wrong. My wife tried to kill my daughter. I'm grateful for the love and care you've given her. Tell me about her. What's her favorite color, food, and sports team?" asks Zion.

"She loves purple, spaghetti, and is a diehard Steelers fan," replies Dominique.

"Oh no! What have you done to my baby? I have to convert her to the Ravens. She's halfway there if she likes purple," jokes Zion.

"It's not happening," says Demetrius, and they all share a good laugh. There's a small knock at the door.

"What's so funny?" asks Sahara as she opens the door. "Hi, Mr. Zion!" Sahara runs to Zion, giving him a big hug and kiss on his cheek. Tears well up in Zion's eyes. "Why are you sad?" asks Sahara.

"I'm not sad. I'm very happy," responds Zion. Dominique wipes the tears from her eyes as her husband rubs his hand across her back.

"Mr. Zion, I have a really cool scar. You want to see it?"

"Yes, but call me Uncle Zion. We're friends, okay?"

"Yes, we're friends," replies Sahara.

"Your parents told me you were big and strong, finishing your physical therapy."

"Yep, and I didn't cry when I got a really big needle either. Do you want to see my cards and balloons from my friends at school? They're in my room," says Sahara.

Zion examines Dominique's and Demetrius' facial expressions. They both nod, giving their approval. Sahara takes Zion by the hand to her room where she entertains him for hours. Life's trials can bring chaos and a laughing calm after the storm.

ACKNOWLEDGMENTS

My sincerest appreciation goes out to Sharon Honeycutt and Jodi McPhee for their superior editorial and interior design skills. Jay Alfred Ferrer, thank you for my initial book cover concept and for bringing it to life. I am deeply indebted to Adrijus Guscia for elevating the concept to an even greater level.

Furthermore, I would not have been able to complete this book without the help of my immediate family and the unconditional love and support that they provided me in the most trying of times.

Lastly, I owe an incalculable debt to God for seeing me through so many storms and for providing me with the grace and mercy necessary for me to be where I am today. To Him I give all the glory!

ABOUT THE AUTHOR

 **Yolanda Soto** is a Delaware native with extensive experience in education, finance, and management. During her adolescence, she discovered her talent for storytelling, and her favorite English teacher, Ms. Andrews, encouraged her to use her overactive imagination. Yolanda creates a wide range of curriculums for financial literacy and literary programs. She has overcome numerous challenges and uses her life experiences to inspire her audience. Yolanda has three lovely daughters: A' Lonna, Tatyana, and Nylah.